BAD BOYS DON'T MAKE GOOD BOYFRIENDS

A LIFE LESSONS NOVEL

MELANIE A. SMITH

WICKED DREAMS PUBLISHING

Published by

WICKED DREAMS PUBLISHING

info@wickeddreamspublishing.com

Boise, ID USA

Edited by Jennifer Gardner

Cover design by Wicked Dreams Publishing

Formatting by Wicked Dreams Publishing

eBook (K) ISBN: 978-1-7328154-0-7

eBook ISBN: 978-1-7330748-9-6

Paperback ISBN: 978-1-7328154-1-4

Hardback ISBN: 978-1-952121-07-4

CONTENTS

"**M**onday morning can eat a buffet of dicks," I groan, slumping my head onto the cool desktop.

"You would know about eating a buffet of dicks." I look up when I hear the voice of Julianna Magnusson, friend, supervisor, tormentor …

"With all due respect, fuck off, Jules," I grumble, rubbing my forehead as she passes by with a loaded medical supply cart and a shit-eating grin.

"Oh, come on, it's not *that* bad." My best friend, Sasha Suvorin, who is sitting next to me, rubs my back gently with one hand while she finishes pulling patient charts with the other.

"Easy for you to say when you probably spent all weekend having orgas—" Sasha claps her hand over my mouth.

"Obviously, I need to remind you that we are *at work*," she hisses.

That's my darling Sasha. Always such a prude. Like people don't know that she and Dr. Hottie are getting it on at every opportunity. The nurse and the doctor. Such a cliché.

And since I'm feeling extra salty this morning, I lick her hand. She pulls it away with a grimace.

"Gross, Becca. Gross."

"Dude, I grew up with four brothers. Licking someone's hand doesn't even show up on the list of the grossest shit I've done."

"I'd be willing to bet that list has more stuff on it from your dating life than from growing up with brothers," she replies with a smirk.

I grin widely, never one to waste an opportunity to shock my oh-so-proper BFF.

"I said 'gross,' not 'kinky.' That's a *whole* other list." I give her a wink and she rolls her eyes, pushing her dark blond ponytail back behind her shoulders.

"And that's my cue to head to the morning

meeting," she replies, rising from the nurses' station desk.

I chuckle softly as I follow her. It's fun watching her squirm, so I never explain to her that none of my dating-related lists are actually all that long. Hers are just that short. Okay, well, maybe mine are a *little* long.

As we walk into the room, she lights up at the sight of her man across the room. And I have to remind myself her lists are probably not as short as they used to be. And mine aren't getting any longer.

He gives her a look that leaves nothing to the imagination. Well, to my imagination. Damn, this dry spell is killing me.

It takes all my strength to focus on the meeting. The chief of our unit, Dr. MacDougall — or Dr. MacBoring, as I like to call him — does his best impression of Charlie Brown's parents at the front of the room, and it's all I can do to stay awake.

"Make sure your chart notes properly reflect ..." *blah, blah, blah,* "and make sure you read the revised policy documentation on ..." *Snore.*

Why do I bother attending, you ask? Besides it being mandatory, even for medical assistants, as soon as it's over, it's open season for the latest gossip and the only time of the day where all the nurses and MAs are in one place.

As the meeting breaks up, I'm not disappointed when Avery Carter, a fellow MA, tugs at my wrist.

"I heard something you might be interested in," she says in a low voice.

I narrow my eyes, knowing Avery is rarely one to give up a juicy piece of gossip without expecting something in return.

"Yeah?"

"Oh, yeah. About that new orderly over in intensive care who you've been crushing on."

My eyebrows shoot up. "Who says I'm crushing on him? Dude's taken. I don't mess with guys with girlfriends."

Avery scoffs. "I prefer women and *I'm* crushing on him. The guy is hot as hell."

I shrug, feigning indifference. Even though she's not wrong. I spent the better part of last month uncharacteristically bummed when I found out the dude was taken. Because *da-yum*. "Hot as hell" doesn't even begin to cover it.

But then I remembered that it's always the best-looking guys who are the worst in bed.

They've never had to work for pussy a day in their lives. You'd think with how much they get, they'd be better between the sheets. But why work on pleasing a woman when she's so eager to please you? No, I'm better off staying away from him. Besides, he screams "bad boy," and everybody knows that bad boys don't make good boyfriends.

Not that I'm exactly looking for a boyfriend. Four horny older brothers with loose lips and seemingly little respect for women have shown me exactly what's going on in a man's brain. And it isn't pretty.

"Sure, he's nice to look at. But I honestly don't care enough to cough up whatever you think you're going to get from me for you to spill the beans."

This is a game we play a lot. One that I usually win.

"Nina told us he's single," Harper Hughes, another MA, pipes up as she joins us.

Avery shoots her a dirty look, at which Harper just shrugs.

"He broke up with his girlfriend?" I ask.

"No, Nina was talking to Cindy, who was the one who said he had a girlfriend in the first place. Turns out she made that up to keep the vultures away," Harper explains. Avery throws her hands up and walks away. Harper chuckles. "She wanted you to cover her shift this Sunday."

"Well, that wasn't going to happen," I reply drily. "Does that mean Cindy struck out?"

Harper grins. "Big time. He wouldn't even talk to her about anything nonwork related. Apparently, it was hilarious. Almost makes me wish I worked in intensive care so I could've watched. Almost."

I huff a short laugh. Most people don't want to work in intensive care or emergency. The cardiac unit here at Rutherford Hospital may have its challenges, but it's not nearly as demanding or stressful. It takes a special kind of person to deal with all that craziness.

Besides, one of the things I enjoy the most about my job is being able to leisurely talk with patients as I prep them for the nurses and doctors. Since we see mostly elderly patients who love nothing more than a good chat, I have all kinds of fun with the old coots. Most of them have been across multiple units for various health issues and have loads of good stories.

They're fantastic sources of gossip and enter-tainment.

"So what do you want for this?" I ask curiously.

Harper blushes. "Nothing. Figured I owed you for … well, you know. All the trouble I caused with Sasha and all."

I give her a look. "Then you should be doing Sasha favors, not me." Not that I super mind.

"I would if she'd let me, but you know her." Harper shrugs.

"Yeah, she's pretty self-sufficient, that one," I agree. "Anyway, thanks. If for nothing else than putting Avery in her place for a minute."

"Anytime," Harper assures me with a smile as we head our separate ways.

As I go about my morning duties, my mind wanders more than usual. Dude is single. But apparently rejected Cindy, who is really pretty. Tall, thin, big blue eyes, corn silk blond hair, and a quiet, waifish quality about her that I think most guys dig. Nothing like my thick, curvy hips that are barely contained by our standard-issue hospital scrubs, the unruly dark brown curls that I keep coiled in a bun at the nape of my neck, and an attitude the size of California. I'm the J.

Lo to her Taylor Swift. But maybe it had nothing to do with looks. Maybe dude's too good for everyone? Guys that hot usually think they are.

I'm still thinking about it that afternoon when Sasha finds me back at the nurses' station.

"You okay?" she asks. I look up to find her staring at me with a furrowed brow, hands on hips.

"Why wouldn't I be?"

"Because you typed the letter 'u' about six hundred times," she replies, pointing at the screen.

"I totally meant to do that," I reply with mock indignation. "It's a passive-aggressive rebuttal to MacDougall's incessant chart notes lecture."

Sasha smirks as she settles into the workstation next to me.

"Yeah, okay. Who is he?"

I heave a sigh, not even wanting to pretend I don't know what she's talking about.

"Vincent DeMarco," I admit.

"Who?" she asks, brows scrunched together.

"The hot orderly," I explain.

"Ah. He has a name."

I give her a look. "Of course he has a name.

But apparently what he doesn't have is a girlfriend."

"And that's a bad thing?" she asks, looking confused.

"No. I'd just put him in the 'has a girlfriend' box in my head," I reply.

"So are you going to go for it then?" she asks. That would sound casual to someone who didn't know her, but I can hear the undertone of excitement. I shoot her a dirty look.

"Why bother? Been there, done that." Her mouth drops open, and I hold up a hand. "Before you can take that the wrong way, I haven't done *him*. But I've been with enough guys like him to know it's just not worth it."

"I don't understand. You were super into the guy before you thought he had a girlfriend," she objects.

"Yeah, that was before I remembered that guys that hot are all talk. It's all, 'Ooh, baby, I'm gonna do things to you you've never even dreamed of before' and 'Damn, girl, I could hit that all night.' Then five minutes later, a little rubbing, and they've come in their pants before you even got to see them naked, much less get off yourself. Nah, not worth it."

Sasha looks nervously down both directions of the hall we're on, checking to see if anyone heard my little diatribe.

"That was … wow."

I shrug. "Just the truth. He'll remain good eye candy. I'll find someone else to have fun with. No biggie."

"If you say so, I just …" Sasha chews on her lower lip nervously.

"What?" I prompt.

She sighs heavily. "I just wish you could have what I have. I know you're not really looking for a relationship or anything, but neither was I. And it's … I mean, I feel like an idiot gushing, but I want that for you too."

I lay a hand over hers. "You want me to be happy," I say, reaffirming the message I know she's trying to send. She nods. "I appreciate that. I *am* happy. Do you remember that time in the sterilization room you lectured me about being happily single? Well, that's where I'm at. I like my life the way it is."

Sasha sucks her lips into her mouth in a way that I know means she has something to say she thinks I won't like. I give her my best "just say it" look and patiently wait for her to spit it out.

"I thought I did too. That's all. I don't mean to belittle what you said. I just … I didn't know I could be *this* happy."

I shake my head and give her a dim smile, trying not to be annoyed. "I'm glad you're happy, Sash. You know I am. Maybe I'll have that someday. Maybe I won't. But I'm cool. I can get my oxytocin rush with some random guy, or a vibrator, or whatever, in the meantime. It's cool. Really."

"Do you really believe that? Because when you say something is 'cool' twice, it's probably not. Just sayin'." She rises and grabs a stack of patient files. "I'll be back."

I stare after her, trying not to be annoyed. I kind of have to admit to myself that she might have a point. Maybe I do want that on some level. But I really don't want all the other bull-shit that comes with it. Because you have to kiss a lot of fucking frogs to find a man worth keeping around.

"Tell me again why we're doing Friday night happy hour *here*?" Jules asks loudly over the music.

"Because there's more to San Diego night life than hoity-toity bars that cater to hospital staff and college students. And after this week, I need to *dance*," I explain loudly, adjusting my black crop top and shaking my shoulders to the beat. It's just a bar with deejay night and a tiny place to shake your thang, but it'll do.

Sasha shoots a nervous glance at Jules, who simply raises her hands in defeat. At least she knows it's pointless to argue with me. With a grin, I grab Sasha by the hands and pull her onto the dance floor behind us.

"Dance like you don't have a man," I shout to her, working my body to the music.

Sasha glances over my shoulder and points at the door. "How about like our coworkers aren't watching?" she shouts back.

I twist my hips and swing around to see Harper and Avery enter. Harper is still in scrubs but, like me, Avery has changed into more casual clothes.

I spin back around and shrug, continuing to let loose while Sasha nervously shuffles from one foot to the other in a horrible imitation of dancing.

"Why do you care so much? C'mon, girl," I grab her hands in mine and make her shimmy along with me. Soon, she's laughing and actually dancing. The girls join us, with even Jules finding her way onto the dance floor and bobbing her head to the music. I shake my head and laugh, pulling at Jules to get her moving.

"I'm too old for this," she shouts while laughing, her gorgeous dark-red hair swinging around her tall, lean frame.

"You're thirty-four, not ninety-four," I say back with a laugh. Just because she's one of our most experienced nurse practitioners doesn't mean she's too old to party. In fact, it means she probably needs to more than any of us. I put my hands over my head and bump her with a hip, causing her hips to sway away from me. Catching on, she sways back and bumps me in time to the music. "That's right, you got this."

She grins at my encouragement. "Old dog," she says, pointing at herself.

"New trick," I tease back, pointing at myself with a wink. "Now we just need to get down and dirty with some boys. Hey, Sash!" I grab Sasha and turn her toward me.

"What?" she shouts.

"Tell your man to get his fine ass over here and bring some of our male coworkers with him. Time to get scandalous up in here."

"I already took care of that," Harper pipes up, pointing toward the tables.

I turn around to see so many bodies in scrubs crowded around the tables we'd been at that it takes me a minute to catch all the faces. Dr. Thompson — Cal — is already making his way over to Sasha with a grin on that fine face of his, while Dr. Franklin stands at the tables making small talk with Zoe and Ethan, two of the cardiac unit nurses. A third cardiac unit nurse —

Mark — hangs at the table next to them with two other guys and a girl. The girl I recognize as Nina, the MA from intensive care that Harper is friends with, but I can't see either of the guys that well as they're both on the far side of the crowd. But my gut tells me Harper is up to something.

I pull on Harper's arm until my mouth is at her ear. "What did you do?" I demand.

She shoots me a guilty look. "I just … invited some people I thought you might want to get to know," she responds lamely.

"A setup? Seriously? This isn't fucking high school, Harper."

She blushes bright red. "Sorry," she says, then leans in so only I can hear her. "I actually like his friend. I thought if you and Vincent hit it off, I could get Mason on his own."

I pull back, unable to keep from laughing. "Oh my god, this *is* high school." I wipe a few tears of laughter from my eyes. It's what I get for being a twenty-six-year-old surrounded by a bunch of newbie MAs in their late teens and early twenties. "Don't you worry about a thing, baby girl, I got you."

I fall back into the beat, circling around

Harper so I can casually observe the guys. Their backs are still to us, but it looks like everyone is on their first rounds of drinks.

"I'm thirsty," I declare, grabbing Harper and Jules and dragging them back toward the tables. Avery follows behind.

Cal and Sasha are at the table with all cardiac unit peeps and Jules joins them, so I drag Harper and Avery over to the table with Mark, Nina, and the others.

"Hey, guys," Nina says, flipping her long dark hair over her shoulder. "We got a couple pitchers of beer. You're welcome to share."

"Thanks," Harper responds. "You remember Avery and Becca?"

"Of course," Nina chirps. "Avery, Becca, these are my friends Mason and Vincent."

"Nice to meet you guys," I pipe back. Avery echoes my sentiment and the guys mumble the same back. Before I end up staring at Vincent, I turn to give Mark a nod. "'Sup, dude."

A giant smile crinkles the corner of his blue eyes. Tall and stocky, his light brown hair is disheveled and his cheeks are red. And judging by the almost-empty pint glass in front of him, I can guess why.

"Becccccaaaaa," he says, much more loosely than usual, pulling me under his arm and giving me a squeeze. He points down at me with his other hand. "This is my homegirl, Becca, guys. She's awesome."

I slip out of his grip, not missing Nina furrowing her brow and taking a slightly possessive step toward Mark. *Interesting.*

"Heh. Thanks," I reply. "Clearly you've got a head start on me, though, so I'd better catch up." I pull three glasses and pour out, handing one each to Harper and Avery. I take a deep drink, checking out Mason as I do. He's probably in his early twenties, average height, with dirty blond hair and brown eyes. Decently muscular. All around a good-looking guy. He and Harper actually kind of have the same coloring and averageness. But then, I have heard that people tend to be attracted to people who look like them.

My eyes flick to Vincent, who is looking out over the crowd. It occurs to me that we have similarities too. Dark hair, dark eyes, thick. He's clearly muscled under the russet-colored T-shirt straining over his chest and upper arms. Damn, those arms with their bulging muscles and tattoos creeping out from under the sleeves. And while I consider myself pretty, this guy is off-the-charts gorgeous with his cut cheekbones, sharp jaw, and perfect olive-toned skin. My girlie bits start to tingle, and I internally bitch-slap myself back to the moment.

"So, Mason, what do you do at the hospital?" I ask, shifting my eyes back to him.

"I'm an MA in emergency," he says shortly. "You?"

"MA in cardiac," I reply just as shortly. "Same as my gorgeous friend, Harper, here." I turn to her and wink, and she pales, looking mortified. I take another sip of beer to hide my smile.

I look up at Vincent to find him staring back at me with an amused look on his face. I stare back, delicately raising an eyebrow. Normally, that'd make guys look away. Not this guy.

"You're new, right?" I ask him. "How are you liking Rutherford so far?"

He shrugs. "It's cool." And his bad-boy image is somewhat belied by his smooth, honeyed voice. Though it makes him that much more attractive, and I want to make him talk more so I can keep that voice in my head for fantasies later.

"He's been a godsend," Nina interjects. "He's one of the only orderlies who actually does what you ask, when you ask."

A light pink tinge graces Vincent's perfect cheekbones. Avery scoots closer to Vincent and says something in his ear. Vincent laughs. Like, really laughs, and I instinctively glare at Avery. Not that she's paying any attention to me. Or that I should care. I've written the guy off, after all. It's probably just the slight competition that always exists between Avery and me. We definitely have a love-hate thing going on. She can be fun, but she can also be a bitch.

I distract myself by chatting with Mark and Nina, leaving Harper free to talk to Mason, which she does, albeit self-consciously. I feel Mark and Nina out a little to see if Mark is into her too and am not surprised to discover that he is. But it doesn't seem like they've done anything about it yet.

"Okay, enough talking," I declare once I figure that out. "I want to see butts on the dance floor." I grab Mark and Nina's hands, shoving them together and toward the dance floor. I suppress my glee when, with a shrug, Mark offers his hand to Nina and she takes it.

I point at Mason and Harper. "You two next," I direct.

Mason shoots Harper an amused look. "Is she always this bossy?"

"Damn straight," I answer for her. "Dance now, thank me later."

Harper gives me a look somewhere between cautiously happy and mortified. I pull her toward me. "He likes you. I can tell. Just do it, girl," I murmur in her ear.

With a deep breath, she pulls a totally willing Mason by the hand. I clap softly as they walk away before realizing I'm now left at a table with Vincent and Avery, who are clearly enjoying their private conversation. And hell if I'm going to encourage them to start bumping and grinding in front of me.

Without a word, I head over to the other table to find that Cal and Sasha have also started dancing, as have Ethan and Jules. A couple of people have hung back to drink and chat, but I'd rather dance than talk. And while I don't have a partner, I don't need one.

I find a spot among my peeps and just go for

it. Sasha finds me quickly, pulling away from Cal so we can all loosely dance together. She's sweet, but I feel bad for interrupting them, so I slink away back to the tables, only to find Vincent by himself.

"Where's Avery?" I ask, pouring myself another pint.

"Phone," he replies shortly, taking a drink of his own beer.

I presume that means she had to make or take a phone call, but I have to laugh at his brevity.

"Dude, shut up, you talk too much," I joke.

He raises a brow at me and I snicker.

"Harper and Avery are friends, right?" he asks, apropos of nothing. Damn, his voice is so sexy it actually makes me shudder.

I set my glass down. "Ooh, a full sentence," I tease. "Yeah. Like, best friends. Why?"

Vincent shrugs. "They're just really different."

"Oh, you mean, since Harper is nice, you thought Avery would be cool?"

Now *I* get his full laugh.

"Something like that."

"Yeah, that's not how girls work, bro," I joke. "She bothering you?"

"Nothing I can't handle."

I snort. "I'm sure you can."

Just then, Mason and Harper reappear. Harper asks me if I need to use the ladies' room, but I decline, so she heads off on her own. Mason and Vincent talk between themselves in low voices, I presume about us girls. I drink my beer, staring out at the crowd, wishing I was dancing.

When Harper returns she tells us that she ran into Avery, who was on her way out. Can't say I'm sad she couldn't stay. Harper darts a look at the guys, clearly reticent to draw Mason's attention back to her.

I set my glass down and dust off my hands dramatically. "Hey, Vincent." The guys stop talking and he looks over at me with a questioning expression. "I need someone to dance with." I step back from the table and extend my hand in invitation.

He continues to stare at me for a moment before glancing back at Mason, who gives him an encouraging look.

"Yeah, okay," he finally replies, rising to follow me. But he doesn't take my hand.

When we start dancing, he doesn't touch me, either. At least we're giving Mason and Harper space. But geez. And he seems really stiff and uncomfortable, though he's clearly got rhythm and, I suspect, some good moves by the sexy roll of his hips and his shoulders as he tries to contain his participation to the smallest movements possible.

I scan the dance floor, noting there are plenty of other single girls, and guys for that matter.

"If you want to find someone else to dance with, it's cool. I just wanted to give Harper and Mason some time alone," I explain.

"You like playing matchmaker, don't you?"

I shrug. "I don't make matches. But I'm happy to give people who I think like each other a little shove in the right direction," I clarify.

"Pretty sure they'd figure it out on their own," he returns with a challenging look.

I smile tolerantly. "Maybe. Maybe not. The first leap is the hardest. Not everyone is brave enough to take the chance. So I help them. You gotta go after what you want sometimes, even if it's scary. Even if you need help to do it."

He shrugs. "I guess."

I laugh and shake my head. "Whatever. Are you gonna actually dance with me or what?"

"I *am* dancing with you."

"No, you're moving ever so slightly from left to right near me," I shoot back. "Have you never really danced with a woman? Or maybe you're just scared to."

"Do you ever not say what's on your mind?" he retorts with an annoyed huff.

I grin, kind of happy that I've gotten under his skin. It feels like good payback for the weeks I spent lusting after him. Not that that was his fault, but still.

"Nope," I reply matter-of-factly. I scan the crowd again, looking for Sasha and Jules. I note that Jules is back at the tables, and spot Sasha and Cal across the floor near Mark and Nina, who are looking awfully cozy. "I'm gonna go dance with my friends."

Vincent levels a look at me and crosses his arms over his chest but doesn't say anything. I shake my head and huff a laugh, giving him a wave before I turn to make my way through the crowd.

That is, until I feel a large hand close around

my wrist. Suddenly, I'm spun around and pulled against Vincent's massive chest. It takes my breath away, literally, as our bodies collide.

I look up into his eyes, warm and rich like melted dark chocolate, and for once I'm speechless.

He doesn't say a word. He wraps his arm around my back, pulling our hips together, his leading mine to the rhythm. It's innocent enough, our fronts melded as he gives in to the music, pulling my body with his to the beat. Just as I thought, he's no beginner at this, and his body works against mine expertly, playing out the sensuality of the song in our movement. But always staying maddeningly just this side of down and dirty.

Still, I let him lead, pushing down the yearning for more. I've already convinced myself not to go there and, despite my starved hormones begging for more, I don't want to encourage him to do something that would make that decision even more difficult to stick to.

But when the song switches to something slower and undeniably hotter, his body automatically switches too. He turns me around, sinking to meld to my body from behind, following my rhythm as I instinctively twist to the beat. His hands find my hips, resting gently as I lean back into him, freeing my mind and body to find my flow. The warm strength he exudes wraps around me as I move, heightening all of my senses.

So when his hands move to the exposed skin of my shoulders, sliding lightly down my arms, every hair on my body stands to attention, warmth shooting across my skin under his touch. Still, I don't overthink it, instead allowing the sensation to add to my oneness with the experience. I lean my head back onto his shoulder as his fingers lace with mine, as our bodies move as one together. Rarely have I danced with someone who could move like him, who fit perfectly behind me, who could keep me totally in the moment.

It makes me wonder, if he can dance like this, make me feel like this with clothes on … *No*. Not going there. Don't need a man who thinks he's all that. Don't need to be dating a coworker. Yep. That's my story, and I'm sticking to it.

So when the song ends, I'm relieved to leave the blissful cocoon that had been dancing with him. Because the curiosity it stirred is just trouble. Vincent DeMarco is just trouble.

"Hey, I need to use the ladies," I tell him, unable to look him in the eye.

He shrugs indifferently, following me as far as the tables, where he goes back to his seat as I head to the restrooms.

I take the opportunity to clean up and take a few deep breaths to control whatever reaction I'd been having to dancing with Vincent. When I return, it's fully locked down.

We all chat for a while and have more to drink. Eventually people start heading home — well, people from the big kids table, anyway. Though I say that like Sasha isn't two years younger than me. But since she's dating a guy nearly ten years older than her and kind of acts like an old lady, if the shoe fits …

She goes home with Cal, and only Ethan is left, so he joins our table. But that once again unbalances the guy-girl ratio, in the other direction this time. Mark and Nina go back to dancing, as do Mason and Harper. And I'm glad to see them all hitting it off.

When Ethan asks me to dance, I don't miss Vincent's complete lack of reaction. Good. I don't have to worry about him getting the wrong idea. To underscore that, I accept, and Ethan and I hit the dance floor.

And I almost immediately regret it. Don't get me wrong, Ethan's a sweetheart, but he's the epitome of the goofy white guy with no rhythm. So instead of enjoying dancing with him for his skills, I instead opt for some over-the-top hilarity, busting out some seriously antiquated dance moves, and we find our groove that way. At some point I start actually having fun. And after a while I'm laughing my ass off at Ethan's attempted moonwalk when Harper taps me on the shoulder.

"Hey, I'm heading out with Mason and Vincent, okay?" she says in my ear.

I give her a questioning look. "Vincent?"

"They came here together. Mason's going to take us both home. Do you need a ride, or are you good?"

My eyes flick up to the tables, where Mason and Vincent stand, clearly waiting for Harper. Vincent's hands are tucked in his jean's pockets and his eyes are floating lazily around the bar, not fixed on anything in particular, his boredom completely evident.

"I'm good," I assure her, my eyes snapping back to hers. "Make sure he drops Vincent off first." I give her a wink.

Harper blushes and nods. "Thanks for everything, Becks."

I give her a quick kiss on the cheek. "I got you, boo. Now go get that cutie pie alone and do everything I would do."

Her look of horror makes me laugh.

"Okay, fine, do *some of* what I would do," I correct.

She bites into her bottom lip and scrunches her nose, clearly self-conscious about her reaction. "That I can do," she promises. "Bye."

I push her away and go back to Ethan. As I do, Vincent's glance lands on me. But I don't turn back around. I'd rather go to sleep alone tonight than chase after a man who has to be coerced into even dancing with me. Even if it was a hell of a dance.

3

"We've got a full schedule today, and Avery is out on personal business. I need you two to cover her check-ins, and I'll get one of our orderlies to handle running laundry and biohazardous waste disposal until she's back. They can do supplies too if you can't keep up." Jules puts her hands on her hips. "That means there isn't time to shoot the breeze. Not with patients. Not with each other. Not with the nurses. Understood?"

Harper and I exchange a glance.

"Sir, yes, sir," I bark, snapping to attention and saluting. Harper stifles a laugh and Jules rolls her eyes.

"Split up her charts and get to it then," Jules

grumbles. "And maybe someday we'll get enough budget to staff so that we're not in dire straits when we're down a single MA." She stalks off without another word, clearly once again displeased with hospital administration. She usually handles stress much better than this, so I can only assume there's something else going on that I don't know about.

In any case, Harper and I immediately set to distributing files. Though we're attempting to sort them so we can physically manage to get them all done, I see one I must have.

I hold up the file marked "Cormac Quinlan Murphy."

"Oh, please, can you take my two o'clock so I can do this one? I love old Irish dudes. They remind me of my Grandpa Dillon," I beg.

"Ha. Sure, why not?" Harper agrees. "Remind me to kill Avery if whatever she's out for isn't really, really serious."

"Only if I don't kill her first," I agree.

We part ways to divide and conquer. The day speeds by, as it always does when we're effectively overbooked. But I'm still looking forward to my Irish grandpa patient when I head into the waiting room, chart in hand.

"Cormac Murphy?" I call expectantly.

To my surprise, a younger man whom I'd pegged as waiting for a relative rises.

"You're Cormac Murphy?" I ask, shocked.

He runs a hand nervously over the stubble on his face.

"That I am," he agrees. "But I go by Quin."

The accent. Oh, the accent. And the way his dark brown hair falls into his cognac-colored eyes … this guy's a total hottie, and he can't be more than thirty.

I clear my throat, getting ahold of myself. "Hi Quin, I'm Becca. Follow me, and we'll get you started," I say, gesturing for him to follow. I get his weight and height, then lead him into exam room five.

I gesture to a chair and take a seat on the rolling stool, setting my tablet up on the desktop. I verify his identity before proceeding, confirming that he's only twenty-eight. Yeesh. That's a good thirty to forty years younger than our average patient. I'm not sure what to think about that. I don't usually have to worry about being attracted to our patients, given their age. But this … oh boy.

"So what brings you in today?" I ask, determined to focus with my fingers poised over my traveling keyboard.

He rubs his chest self-consciously. "I'd had a weird, dull pain in the chest for a while. Then last week I got a really sharp pain and some tingling in my arm. I went in to see my physician, who said my blood pressure is high, but he wanted to make sure that it wasn't something worse. Just as a precaution," Quin explains.

It's hard to focus on his words, given his accent and the adorableness that is him. But I push through and document it all, asking him a few more clarifying questions, what medications he's on, and so forth.

"Okay, I'm going to take your blood pressure now," I say on a breath. I grab the cuff, wrapping it around his bicep and focus on inflating it and listening for the blood flow points. His eyes watch me curiously, making it even harder to concentrate. "Yep, you're a little high." I undo the cuff.

"Forgive me, but aren't you a little bit beautiful to be a nurse?" he asks.

I look at him, eyebrows raised.

"Oh my god," he says, turning red. "Young. I meant *young* to be a nurse."

I burst out laughing. "I'm a medical assistant," I reply. "Though I'm twenty-six, so not too young, or beautiful for that matter, to be a nurse."

"I'm so sorry," he says, putting a hand over his face. "I feel like a complete fool. Is there any way we can pretend that I never said that?"

"It's okay," I assure him. "It happens. It's no big deal."

I finish entering some notes and close the tablet.

"I hope I didn't make you uncomfortable. I imagine you get hit on all the time," he says.

"Well, I do," I admit. "But it's a bit different coming from an attractive guy my age rather than the usual patient, who could easily be my grandfather."

The look of hope on his face is priceless.

"Dr. Carson will be in momentarily," I say, turning toward the door.

"It was nice to meet you, Becca," he replies with a grin.

"You too, but I'll be back when the doctor is done with you," I respond. And I can't help giving him a little wink as I leave. Even though I know I shouldn't. But fuck it. That guy is hot. And he called me beautiful.

So I'm not sorry to have to go back a little more than half an hour later. Dr. Carson has ordered the usual echo and stress tests, so I grab the necessary paperwork as I head back in.

After I've provided him the forms and scheduled his appointment, I'm about to walk him out when he rises and stops in front of the closed door.

"Would you want to get coffee with me sometime?" he asks tentatively.

I look up, realizing he's quite a bit taller than me. And that while it's not the most professional thing to do, I honestly don't want to say no.

"I'd like that," I reply.

"Excellent," he says with a grin. He fishes a card out of his pocket. "Here's my cell number. Give me a call, we'll set something up soon."

I take it, sliding it into my shirt pocket. "I'll do that."

"ARE YOU NUTS? YOU CAN'T DATE A PATIENT," Sasha hisses at me from her usual late afternoon position at the workstation next to mine.

"Says who? There's not a rule," I reply. "I checked."

"God, you sound just like Cal," she says.

"And look how that worked out," I point out.

She gives me a stern look. "This is different."

"How, exactly?"

She opens and closes her mouth a few times, clearly unable to come up with a reply.

"Yeah, that's what I thought. I'm going to consider this a perk that balances out a lot of the bullshit I have to deal with getting hit on by skeevy old dudes."

"Fine, it's your reputation, your job. Do what you want."

"I always do," I retort with a wink.

"Not always," she parries back.

"What's that supposed to mean?"

She snorts. "You did a complete one-eighty on the hot orderly. You were all about him for weeks, then suddenly you're over it. Then you guys dance-fucked at our little after-work thing last Friday, but now you're acting like nothing happened."

"Did you just say '*dance-fucked*'? And while at work?" I ask, letting out a laugh of disbelief. "That might be the best thing I've ever heard you say, Sash. Say it again."

She glares at me and wrinkles her nose. "Don't be a pain in the ass," she snips.

"Oh, I live to be a pain in the ass," I tease. "But I'm acting like nothing happened because nothing did happen. We danced, which, by the way, I literally had to talk him into doing. I was dead right about him. He knows how hot he is, and he's totally weird and antisocial to boot. Not. Interested."

Sasha looks like she wants to argue with me, then thinks better of it. "Fine. So what about this Quin guy?"

With a grin, I proceed to tell her everything, trying to get her as excited about this as I am. But Sasha's a tough nut, and I'm unable to convince her that going out with Quin is a good thing. Guess I'll just have to prove her wrong.

"Irish coffee? Really?"

"What?" I ask indignantly. "We're in an Irish bar. Why's that weird?"

Quin laughs and shrugs. "Suit yourself. I guess I didn't imagine booze when I asked you out for coffee. Especially not on a Thursday night."

"Then you shouldn't have brought me to a bar," I reply with a grin.

"Fair enough, lass. I do love this place, though. About as close as you'll get to a real Irish pub stateside."

"When did you move here?" I ask.

He grips his actual cup of coffee in both hands. "Nigh on three years now."

"Is it too personal to ask why you left?" One of the few times I'll hedge my questions is on a first date. Who says I can't be polite?

"Not at all," he assures me with a smile. "It was a job opportunity. The right job at the right time."

"Do you miss Ireland?"

"Ach, no. I'm in love with California. It's beautiful here. And getting more beautiful by the minute," he replies with a wink.

"So what does a cybersecurity data engineer do, exactly?" I muse out loud.

Quin laughs heartily. "Do you really want to know? Because I'm afraid it bores most people."

"The Cliff's Notes version then?" I suggest, taking a sip of the deliciously intoxicating coffee.

"I purposely try to find ways to attack my company's website, software, that sort of thing. To see what someone trying to do damage could get away with. Then I fix the things I find."

"Well, you made that sound very simple and unboring," I commend him.

"Oh, good," he replies. "So do you have designs on being a nurse, or do you plan to stay just a medical assistant?"

"Is there something wrong with being a medical assistant?" I ask archly.

His ears tinge red. "No, not as such. Just wondering what your career advancement plans are."

"I love my job. Well, as much as anyone can love a job," I reply with a shrug. It's a nonanswer, really, but it was kind of an insulting question. Though I try not to dwell on his implication, choosing instead to move on. We start talking about music, movies, and anything else to find common ground, which there's enough of, thankfully.

By the end of the evening I've decided that he's nice enough but despite being enjoyable to look at, I'm not super attracted to him. And I definitely don't see it going anywhere after the career advancement comment. Don't like me the way I am? Next.

But it might not be a total loss. As we walk out later that evening, he sees me to my car. "Can I see you again?" he asks, standing a polite distance away.

I step toward him, placing a hand on his chest and looking up at him. "That depends," I reply. Though him asking tells me he's not very good at reading between the lines and body language. But he might be good for ending this damn dry spell.

"On?" he asks, his breathing picking up.

I grip the front of his shirt and go up on my toes, pressing my mouth to his. It's … nice. Not spectacular, but not bad either. I pull back and he grins at me.

"I'm free Saturday night," I say.

"Grand," he replies with a grin. "Talk later?"

I nod, unlocking my car. "'Night, Quin."

"'Night, Becca."

I drive home with the radio blasting as usual. It keeps me from thinking too hard about anything. When I lie down to sleep that night, I'd like to say I'm thinking about Quin. But I'm just not. Life would be so much easier if I were.

4

---

*A*very finally returns to work on Friday. Apparently, a close cousin of hers died unexpectedly. So, you know, valid excuse. But it means there's now enough downtime that things are on the boring side. At least I have time to fill Sasha in on my so-so date. She's even less enthused after hearing his comments about my "career plans," or lack thereof, in his opinion anyway. Can't say I disagree. Still, might not be a total loss. But that aside, the day drags on, seemingly never-ending.

That is, until that afternoon, when the mechanical doors between the cardiac unit and the rest of the hospital open to Vincent, navigating a patient in a wheelchair.

He stops at the nurses' station counter, plopping down a clipboard.

"Transfer," he grunts.

"Loquacious as usual, Mr. DeMarco," I comment drily, taking the clipboard.

"You know my last name," he replies with an uncharacteristic smile.

I shrug nonchalantly, rising to take over. "Rumor mill," I grunt back in the same tone he'd used to start, then greet the fairly out-of-it elderly woman in the chair quietly before starting to wheel her toward an in-patient observation room where she'll await surgery. Vincent heads back down the hall, punching the button to open the doors.

"Enchanting as usual, *Ms. Dillon*," he says with a wink. "See you at happy hour."

"Wait, what?"

But he's already gone.

As soon as I've settled the patient and gotten a nurse in to hook up her Hep-Lock, I hunt down Harper. I find her in the supply room, restocking the shelves.

"Harper, why did Vincent just drop off a patient and say, 'See you at happy hour'?" I demand.

She looks up, clearly confused. "We're still doing happy hour after work, aren't we?" she asks.

"Sure, of course, it's Friday. But why is Vincent coming?" I persist.

Harper shrugs. "Why wouldn't he? Mason will be there. They're best friends, after all."

"So he's just part of our group now?"

"I mean … things are going really well with Mason and me. So, yeah, I think he is. He's actually a really chill guy, Becks, you just need to give him time to get past the quiet and stand-offish phase."

"You've been hanging out with him," I gasp accusatorily.

"A little," she admits, blushing. "I hung out at Mason's last night and he was there."

A catlike grin splits across my face. "Yeah? And what happened after he left?"

Harper blushes furiously, and I do a little happy dance on the spot.

"Get it, girl," I squeal.

"Shhhhh," Harper whispers. "I'm trying not to broadcast it until, well, there's something to broadcast. He hasn't exactly asked me to be his girlfriend or anything."

"Well, lock that shit down, because you know news like that isn't going to stay quiet for long," I respond. "Not that I'm going to tell anyone." She looks at me disbelievingly. "Seriously. Cross my heart." And I actually cross my heart.

She gives me another look. I put my hands on my hips and give her a look back.

"Okay, fine, I believe you," she finally says, cracking up.

"Good. Now. How was it?" I demand.

As if she's making up to me for adding to our group without warning, she gives me every last juicy detail. I soak it up like a desert in the rain. Lord knows I'm experiencing a drought.

So I'm considerably less pissed at her when I show up for happy hour that evening, changed into jeans and a blue knit cap-sleeve crop top, my curls loose and flowing for once. I have to keep it tied back so much it gives me a headache, and we're not dancing this time, only drinking, so no need to wear it up.

I ended up stuck at work longer than I'd planned, so everyone is there already, even Cal, who almost always works later than anyone in the unit. It's all the usual suspects minus Zoe, who just went on vacation with her partner to the Maldives. Lucky ducky. And of course, Vincent and Mason are there, as well as Mark and Nina. Mark has always been spotty on showing, but it seems now he and Nina are a thing, they're both going to be regulars too.

I try to suppress my frown as everyone greets me. I'm happy for them, but it seems like everyone in our group is pairing off. No pressure.

Since I'm last in, I end up in a chair just off the booth they're in, not particularly included in any of it. And even though Vincent is too far to talk to me, I somehow get the sense he's purposely avoiding even looking at me. Which is fine, because all I really want to do is drink. Jules, who sits next to me, finally brings me into the conversation, but then backs off as she senses I'm feeling grumpier than usual.

I watch Sasha and Cal whispering together as I drink my second Manhattan. My "I'm happy for them" mantra starts to falter a little as I realize how much I miss my best friend. We used to meet up for drinks after work outside of our usual weekly happy hour, but that hasn't been happening lately. On top of my massive involuntary dating hiatus — one I won't consider broken until I see some action — and I realize suddenly why I'm so grumpy.

"Hey, Jules," I say, nudging her in the side. "I'm going to go get some air. Be back."

"You okay?" she asks softly.

I nod. "Yeah, I'm cool. Just a long week."

"You should go home then, rest up. You're on again tomorrow, so you're going to need it."

I roll my eyes. Like I needed the reminder. "Thanks, but I'm going to need more to drink to be relaxed enough to go to sleep tonight. I'll be back. Promise."

As I rise to leave, I notice Vincent watching me. I don't bother giving him a second glance, instead continuing on my way and heading for the side entrance that's hardly ever used. It leads to a wide alley with a couple of outdoor tables that I'm sure are full on the weekends, but not so much on weeknights. Especially since there's a huge dumpster just a little farther down the alley.

I sink into one of the chairs, stretching my short legs out onto another. I twist in place, trying to relieve some of the tension in my limbs and back. Working in a hospital is hard on the body, and some days I feel it more than others. Today is one of those days.

"You shouldn't be out here after dark on your own."

I look behind me to see Vincent coming out of the side entrance, and I roll my eyes. What the hell is he doing out here? He can't be weird and aloof somewhere else? He closes the door behind him and sinks into a chair on the other side of the table I'm sitting at.

"I'm a big girl. I can handle it."

Vincent levels an impatient look at me. "All the same, I think I'll stick around if that's cool with you."

So now he gives a shit? This guy needs to make up his mind.

But I just shrug indifferently. "Suit yourself." I twist again, trying to crack my back.

"Rough day?" he asks.

"Rough month."

"I feel you. Come here." He stands, gesturing for me to join him.

I rise, and he gathers me in his arms.

"What are you doing?" I ask, pulling back. First he can't even touch me enough to dance with me, now he wants to hold me? Confusing much?

"Just shut up and trust me," he grumbles. "Stay loose."

Against my better judgment, I relax in his arms. He balls his fists together behind my back and pulls sharply toward himself. An immense crack echoes through the alley and a sense of relief washes through my body.

"Holy fucking shit, that was amazing," I groan as the ache seeps out of my back. I look up at him. "Thank you."

He drops his arms and takes a step back. "No problem." He shoves his hands in the pockets of his jeans self-consciously but doesn't back away further or sit back down.

"What else do you have in your bag of tricks?" I tease.

He smirks. "What else hurts?"

I bark a sharp laugh. "Nothing that you can help me with."

"You sure about that?" he asks.

"Pretty sure," I reply, looking up at him firmly and crossing my arms over my chest. I can't decide if I'm laying down a challenge or simply stating fact.

He steps back toward me, leaning in. "I think you might be surprised."

I raise an eyebrow. "And I think guys like you are all talk." Hmmm. Definitely a challenge.

That gets a derisive laugh out of him. "You don't know anything about me."

"I know that you're all over the fucking map. You're moody and withdrawn. I know that I really don't want to be attracted to you."

"But you are."

I throw my hands up. "Yes. Happy?"

"Not really."

I blanch at his words, not sure if he means that he's not happy that I'm attracted to him or that he's not happy in general.

"And why's that?"

"Because I already knew that."

"Pfff," I scoff.

"If it makes you feel better, it's not just you. You don't take shit and you speak your mind. Gotta say, as much as I don't want to, I find that pretty fucking hot."

I give him a skeptical look, fighting a blush from his compliment-slash … insult? "How do you know I don't take shit?" I ask back, a challenge in my tone.

He smirks. "You just made my point," he replies with a chuckle.

"Okay, fine," I allow. "What else do you think you know?"

His brow furrows and he steps toward me. While his eyes sweep over my face, I question whether I'm imagining the tension that's sprung up between us.

"You sure you want me to answer that?" he finally asks.

I swallow hard. "Yes?" I want to kick myself when it comes out sounding like a question, but he has me all kinds of nervous.

And I'm completely thrown off when suddenly, he grabs my hand, pulling me down the alleyway and around the corner to the back of the bar before I can so much as react.

He shoves me up against the wall, his face inches from mine, his eyes full of fire. It freezes me in place.

"I think I know what you really need right now," he grinds out as if the words are being tortured out of him. "And I'm going to fucking give it to you."

In a flash, his mouth descends on mine, his teeth suckling at my lip as he presses his body against me. I don't know if it's the surprise of it all or because it's so fucking good that I don't resist. It's the spectacular kiss I'd been looking for from Quin last night. No. It's a kiss that pretty much trumps every kiss, possibly ever. Filled with hunger, desire. And he's right: It's what I want from him, what I need right now. But where the fuck did this come from? How did he even know? And why is he giving it to me? Better question: Why am I letting him?

His hand reaches between my legs, stroking me through my jeans … and I stop caring why. My arms wrap around his neck, my tongue pressing against his lips. He opens to me, and we explore each other's mouths with a ferocity and urgency that would usually have me tearing off a man's clothes in a less public place. Clearly, he feels the same, as his fingers undo the button on my jeans, unzipping them enough to slip his hand down, under my panties, to the wetness that has bloomed between my thighs.

I don't stop him. I'm not sure I could if I wanted to. Not that I want to, even though this came out of nowhere. Even though this makes no sense. Even though this is everything I thought I didn't want. My body is screaming for release, screaming for his touch, and that's all that matters in this moment.

He moans into my mouth as his fingers find their slippery target. My moan follows his as he circles it with his thumb before slipping his fingers inside me.

He wastes no time, working me hard, his mouth pulling at mine until, in what feels like moments, I'm coming apart, choking back the groans of pleasure from the much-needed orgasm that flows through me. I slump my forehead against his shoulder, letting him support me as the pleasure takes over.

When my muscles start to relax, he withdraws, flicking my sensitive nub on the way and sending one last surge through me. I slump against the wall as he gives me a final, gentle kiss before withdrawing completely.

"Okay, maybe you know a thing or two. Anything else you know that you want to share?" I tease, looking up at him.

"That that's all I've got for you."

He turns away, allowing me to right my clothing. And my head. For whatever reason, he decided to jump me just then. But that's it. I'd be upset if I'd expected anything in the first place.

But I didn't — exactly the opposite — so I don't question him further. Why would I? He's right. I had already decided I don't want anything from him. Though somehow he knew exactly what I needed anyway. And gave it to me. Damn, did he give it to me. One minute he can't stand to touch me, the next he's making me orgasm in two minutes flat. This guy is seriously confusing. Probably best that it starts and ends on a good note.

I lay a hand on his arm, and he turns his head to look at me. "Well, if nothing else, that was pretty damn memorable. Definitely the hottest thing I've ever done. Or, had done to me, as it were."

He gives me a smirk. "Surprised?"

"Completely," I admit freely. "Thank you."

He considers me for a moment with his dark gaze. "You're welcome," he finally replies slowly, reaching out and tugging at a crazy curl. "You should wear your hair down more."

I blink up at him, again astounded by the puzzle that is Vincent DeMarco. When I don't respond, he pulls me along back to the side entrance.

"I have to go," he says.

"Seriously? You're just going to give me an orgasm and bail? What am I going to tell everyone?"

"I really don't care what you tell them."

"So I can tell them you finger-fucked me in the alley then decided to take off?"

He grins widely. "Are you really going to tell them that?"

"Hell, no," I scoff. I can't begin to explain what just happened to myself, much less to other people.

He lets out a short laugh. "Bye, Becca."

And then he walks away without waiting for a response.

"Well, that was the weirdest fucking thing that's ever happened to me," I mutter under my breath as I watch him round the corner and disappear.

When I go back in, everyone is still chatting and drinking, clearly oblivious to what just happened. But why would they be anything but?

"Feeling better?" Jules asks as I slide back into my chair.

"Much, thanks," I say, trying to keep my expression neutral.

"Where's Vincent? He said he was going to sit outside with you," Harper asks.

"He decided to go home," I say as casually as I can.

"Scared him off, huh?" Avery quips.

I spread my hands out and smile. "Guess so."

I notice Sasha, who is on Jules' other side, give me a funny look and my smile falters. I shake my head as lightly as I can and she relents. But I know she's perceptive and more tuned into me than I often give her credit for. And I'm going to have some explaining to do later.

For now, I have another drink, considerably more relaxed than I was. Though way, way more confused.

5

"*I*'m not telling you at work, Sasha, so stop asking."

"Holy shit. Hell has officially frozen over." Sasha leans back in her chair.

"Brunch. Tomorrow. Then I'll be able to tell you about my second date with Quin at the same time," I promise. And maybe that'll give me time to figure out what the hell happened. Scratch that. I don't think there's any figuring out Vincent, or his motivations. Either way, she's going to think I'm such a slut.

Why does that thought make me laugh?

"What's so funny?" she asks suspiciously.

"I'll tell you tomorrow," I say with a chuckle. "But I'm glad we're getting together. I miss you. Is that weird since I see you every day?"

"No, I miss you too," she assures me. "Sorry I've been so …"

"Orgasmic?" I tease.

"You're incorrigible."

"And you love me."

Sasha rolls her eyes but still smiles. "Yeah, yeah, yeah."

I go back to inputting patient data, unable to keep from smiling. Vincent is a fucking orgasm miracle worker. I can't remember ever feeling so relaxed for so long after one. And here I thought he hated me.

I should be pleasantly surprised, but the more I think about it, the more I just don't get it. So I try not to think about it. No sense spoiling my good mood.

"Well, whatever happened, you look pretty damn happy," Sasha remarks after a few minutes.

I look up to find her staring at me.

"Sure am," I reply with a wink.

"And you still won't tell me why?"

"Damn, girl. I've never seen you so curious. Keep asking. I'm really enjoying this," I tease her. It's quite the reversal. Sasha is so reserved, I'm usually the one trying to drag stuff out of her. Guess now she gets to see what that's like.

"Fuck you."

Hmm. Guess she doesn't like getting a taste of her own medicine. I blow her a kiss and return to work with a cackle. She'll live. Though I can't wait to see her reaction tomorrow. I swear sometimes that I do a lot of the things I do just to see how Sasha will react later. Well, maybe not quite, but it's still a huge perk. She's just so easy to shock. And apparently so eager to be.

Here's hoping my date with Quin tonight goes better than I expect, so I can really shock the shit out of her tomorrow. Though the closer it gets, the less I find myself looking forward to it. I've dated around, but something about being with Vincent yesterday has me shook. Don't get me wrong, I heard the boy, loud and clear. That was all. And I don't want more from him.

Who am I kidding? Of course I want more fantastic orgasms. Just without the side of WTF. But now that I've been reminded what real attraction feels like, going out with Quin seems like settling. Or maybe I'm just expecting too much? I don't know. I really have to stop all this thinking bullshit.

"Wow, you look beautiful," Quin says as I meet him in front of my building.

I spin, the light skirt of my little black dress flaring dramatically. "Why, thank you. You look quite handsome yourself," I reply, eyeing his fitted black slacks and light blue button-front shirt. He definitely cleans up well.

"Your chariot awaits," he says, gesturing to the car behind him.

With a chuckle, I approach, and he opens the door, helping me into the passenger seat before going around and climbing in the driver's side.

"Where are we going?" I ask curiously.

He flashes a grin. "You'll see. It's not far."

"Oooh, a surprise. I love surprises."

"Good, because I'm full of them," he replies with a wink as he pulls into traffic.

"Is that so?" I ask teasingly.

"You'll see," he says with a self-assured grin. "You really do look lovely tonight."

"Thanks, you clean up pretty good too," I reply.

"Your hair is … something. Do you ever straighten it?" he asks.

I raise an eyebrow. "I love my hair. It's as crazy as I am."

He huffs out a breath somewhere between a laugh and a scoff. Strike one of the evening. Still, I decide not to pull at that thread and let the conversation move swiftly on.

We make small talk on the way, and a few minutes later we pull up to the restaurant. And I realize I spoke too soon. It's an oyster bar. And I might be the only person in San Diego who doesn't eat seafood. The mere smell makes me sick to my stomach. But mostly … I'm pretty sure I mentioned that over coffee earlier this week.

"Just wait, they have the most amazing food," he gushes as he parks the car.

"I hate to be a party pooper, but I don't actually eat seafood," I say plainly, not bringing up that I almost certainly already mentioned this.

He waves a hand dismissively. "I'm sure they have other things on the menu. I've been dying to eat here all week." He gets out and I sit for another moment, contemplating being *that bitch*. But fuck it. I can survive one meal, right?

Wrong. As soon as we walk in, the smell of fish hits me like a brick wall of vomit waiting to happen. I lay a hand firmly on Quin's forearm.

"I really can't do this," I insist. "The smell —"

"No, really? It can't be that bad," he says, cutting me off with a disappointed look.

"It is. There's a great Italian restaurant just across the street, though," I suggest, trying to breathe as little as possible. Strike two. The fact that he's not immediately turning around and walking out is starting to piss me off.

"Ach, I'm not a big fan of Italian. Maybe we can find someplace else to eat around here."

I huff a laugh. "Dude, we're in the middle of *Little Italy*. We're literally surrounded by Italian restaurants." I manage to control myself enough not to ask who the fuck doesn't like Italian food. "We can drive somewhere else if you want, I just need to get out of here. Now."

He stares at me for a minute. A minute too long. I turn on my heel and exit the restaurant, gulping down the fresh evening air once I'm outside.

Quin approaches from behind me, grumbling and starting back toward the car. "Well, no need to be dramatic. Let's go then."

Oh. No. He. Didn't.

Strike. Fucking. Three.

You do not tell a half Puerto Rican, half Irish-Italian woman that she's being dramatic. That's three cultures of fiery women who will tear you to shreds.

It's on.

I cross my arms over my chest.

"How big is your dick?" I call after him.

Quin stops and turns back, his eyes wide, his mouth hanging open. "Excuse me?"

"How. Big. Is. Your. Dick?" I repeat slowly. "Is it as big as your *cojones*? Because you've got some pretty big fucking ones to talk to me like that."

He crosses the small distance between us. "Lord, woman, we're in public, keep your fecking voice down," he whispers angrily.

"I think I won't," I reply back at normal volume. "And I'd ask you to apologize for being a world-class prick, but that's not going to change the fact that you are. Or that I'm so done. Bye now."

"Yeah, and you're a classless whore," Quin calls after me.

I shake my head and laugh at the irony. Sorry, dude, if you're yelling after someone that they're a classless whore, you're pretty much describing yourself.

As I walk away, I realize that the restaurant next door to the seafood place is a fucking dessert restaurant. Now we're talking.

I open the door angrily, only to get inside and find it's not just a dessert restaurant, it's a *build your own dessert* restaurant. My fury evaporates when I realize that thanks to that asshole, I might have just found heaven. Who even knew this was a thing? But as tempting as that option sounds, they also have chocolate crêpes on the menu. So that's pretty much happening.

I get my food and sit at a table outside, people-watching while I eat. The crêpes are ridiculous. A delicate chocolate pastry wrapped around chunks of brownie and fudge, with chocolate whipped cream on top. This night didn't turn out so bad after all.

I'm downing a glass of water to cut the richness when I hear my name. I look up to see Vincent, across the street, coming out of the

Italian restaurant with a plastic bag in hand. He waits a moment until there's a break in traffic, then jogs across the street. Time seems to slow as I watch him come toward me. It's like a fucking episode of *Baywatch*. Except with leather and tattoos.

"Hey," he says, stopping at the table.

"Hey," I reply. "Fancy meeting you here."

He shrugs. "Just grabbing some takeout."

I gesture to the seat next to me. "You're welcome to join me. I'm drowning my sorrows."

"I have just the thing for that." He sets his bag down and shrugs out of his black leather jacket, much to my dismay, and puts it on the back of the chair before sitting down. Though the clear view of his huge biceps doesn't hurt much either.

He digs through the bag and produces a foil-wrapped package. He opens it to reveal a humongous piece of garlic bread sliced neatly into slivers.

"Really?" I ask with a laugh. "How does that help?"

"All sorrows are less with bread," he replies cryptically.

"Ooookay," I say, reluctantly taking a piece.

"Not sure how this'll go with chocolate crêpes, but what the heck, why not?"

Vincent smirks at me. "It's a line from *Don Quixote*," he explains. "And everything goes with garlic bread."

I give him a skeptical look, holding back a remark about his unexpected reading habits. So I just roll my eyes and take a bite. It's delicious. And while it totally clashes with the flavor of the crêpes, can't say I mind.

"Could you be any more Italian-American?" I joke.

"Am I wrong?" he returns with another smirk.

I narrow my eyes at him. "Not about the bread."

He doesn't take the bait. Instead, he pulls out a takeout container and starts in on the biggest hunk of lasagna I've ever seen.

"So you live around here?" I ask, going back to my crêpes.

"Yup," he says around a mouthful.

"What, no wild Saturday night plans?"

He shakes his head. "My best friend is busy fucking your best friend. Takeout and Netflix were my only plans for the night."

"Harper isn't my best friend," I correct him. I wonder quietly about his use of "were."

"Okay, fine, your friend," he allows. "You look nice. Why are you all dressed up?"

I eye him as I take the last bite of my food. I chew slowly. I'm not afraid to tell him, I just want to make him wait for it. But unfortunately he seems totally unperturbed. As usual, I guess.

"I had a date," I finally respond.

He laughs. "Well, that must've gone really well," he says sarcastically.

I stare at him for a minute. And I realize this guy is way more on my level than Quin. At least, when he's not being confusing as fuck. But really. We have similar jobs. He actually seems to pay far more attention to my words and signals than Quin ever did, despite having talked way more with Quin. And Vincent likes my hair. And Italian food, though, duh. Even more important, neither of us is looking for a relation-ship. And he gave me one of the best orgasms of my life. Maybe he's not the stuck-up, selfish jerk I'd pegged him to be. A complete enigma, yes. But perhaps I can salvage what's left of this evening.

"Worse than the first, for sure," I reply.

His eyebrows raise. "Wow, a second date. And he blew it? His loss."

"What makes you think he blew it?"

"Because I have eyeballs."

"Cute. I'm more than just a body, you know."

He drops his fork and looks up at me. "I know that, Becca. I wish I didn't." He closes up his food container and packs it back into the bag. "I should go."

"Why do you always bail like that?" I ask bluntly.

"I like to keep things simple."

I laugh. "Then you shouldn't have finger-fucked me in a dark alley," I point out.

He blows out a breath and drops back into his seat reflexively. "What do you want from me?" he asks quietly into his hands.

"I just want to know who the fuck you are," I snap. "I mean, there was 'cold and aloof' Vincent who wouldn't even dance with me. Then there was 'smoking hot' Vincent who made grinding magic on the dance floor. Then there was 'whatever' Vincent who ignored me the rest of the night after that. Then 'friendly' Vincent who wanted to see me at happy hour.

Then 'sweet' Vincent who complimented my hair and fixed my back. Then 'off the charts sexy' Vincent who gave me the best fucking orgasm I've ever had completely out of nowhere. Then 'that's it, I've got to go' Vincent who just disappeared like it was nothing. Then there was 'casual and chatty' Vincent. And now we're back to 'disappearing act' Vincent. Which of these dudes are you, really? No. Never mind. That's not what I really want to know. What I really want to know is *why*? Why get me off when most of the time you don't seem to want to have anything to do with me and, by your own admission, you're not looking for this to be anything?"

He huffs a dry laugh. "That's not what you really want to know," is his only response. Then he leans back in his chair with an arrogant smile.

"Seriously? Fine. What do I really want to know?" I ask, folding my arms over my chest and leveling an icy glare at him.

His grin widens and he leans forward on his elbows, looking at me with a glint in his dark, beautiful eyes. "You want to know if I'll do it again."

My throat constricts. And so do other parts

of me. He's not wrong. The bastard does have me pretty hot and bothered, on just about every level. Damn him.

"Dude, you're the one who wanted to keep things simple. If we can do it without the multiple personalities, I might be up for that. Because I like to keep things simple too. Otherwise, no thanks."

I rise, tossing my napkin onto my plate, totally disgusted with the whole night. Fucking men. Can't a girl just get a good lay without all the drama?

"Where are you going?"

"Home. To get myself off. Everything else is too much fucking trouble."

***

"You *DIDN'T*," Sasha gasps.

"Damn fucking straight I did. I left that confusing motherfucker there with his mouth hanging open like the idiot he is," I reply vehemently. "Now, tell me something to restore my faith that not all men are clueless morons. How are you and Cal?"

Sasha snorts. "Oh, please, you know better

than anyone that even he can be as clueless as the rest of them," she reminds me. "But he's good. We're good."

"That's it? 'We're good'? No juicy details for your bestest big sis?" I tease.

"You know I don't talk about that stuff," she says, turning bright red. "Besides, I don't want to rub it in your face."

"Mmm, I could use to have some things rubbed in my face," I say with a sigh. It gets exactly the reaction I expected, as Sasha pulls a face.

"Eww."

"Oh, come on, you know you like it when he does. Admit it, girl."

Sasha turns full-on crimson and I let out an evil cackle.

"I'm just messing with you, boo," I assure her. "Unclench. I won't make you admit you like it." I give her a wink that says, *But we both know you do*. Because I know her. Otherwise she wouldn't have blushed so hard.

"Not to change the subject …" Sasha says.

"But to totally change the subject …" I mimic.

"Yes, to totally change the subject," she

admits with a laugh. "What's up with Jules? She's been totally MIA lately."

"End of the fiscal year," I remind her.

"Oh. Shit."

April is Rutherford Hospital's fiscal year-end. Which means Jules, being on the board as head nurse practitioner of the cardiac unit, spends most of her time arguing for more budget. Something she is equally passionate about and loathes. Because it never ends well.

"Maybe we can do something nice for her. Take her to a spa or something next weekend," I suggest.

"Funny, I was thinking we could do something nice for *you*," Sasha admits with a small smile. "You've been so all over the place, Jules suggested clubbing a couple weeks back, but I hadn't been able to circle back around with her to make plans."

"You guys want to go clubbing with me?" I ask, completely shocked. It's one of my favorite things, but my two best friends in the world aren't so into that scene. Harper will go with me occasionally, but now that she's preoccupied it hasn't happened in a long time. Which is also why I haven't gotten any real action in so long, because it's my main go-to to relieve the sexual tension. All sexiness, no messy relationship aftermath.

"If you want. Yes, that was the plan."

"Awww, you guys are so sweet. You know I'm not about to say no to that."

"Good," she says folding her hand over mine. "It's a girl date."

6

"We missed you at happy hour," Jules says as we're standing in line at the club. She looks phenomenal in a fitted yet still somehow conservative black dress that wraps fully around her slender neck, completely covering those beautifully shaped boobies of hers, then hugging her tall, thin frame to just below the knee. Her matched black heels put her over six feet, totally towering over me and Sasha. Though as good as she looks, I can see the exhaustion in her face.

"Yeah, I just needed a break from … that group," I say awkwardly. Since it's the first time I've seen Jules with just us girls for more than a few weeks, I realize she has no clue what's been going on.

Sasha shoots me a pointed look.

"All right, all right. Since we'll probably be waiting a while …"

I purposely "ran late" to avoid this conversation. But I might as well get it over with. Well, the short version anyway. So I take a deep breath in, then let it all spill out in one quick diatribe. I tell her everything. About Vincent, Quin … more Vincent. And by the time I'm done talking I'm even more over it than I already was.

"But we all look sexy as fuck. So let's just have some fun, okay?" I finish, letting out a huge breath.

The line shifts forward, and we move with it. Jules is silent and Sasha plays with her skirt next to me. I look her up and down, once again admiring the clingy, silvery fabric of her strapless dress. Her hair is even up, with little dark blond wisps framing her made-up face. She almost never dresses up, and she really does look good. Mind, not as good as I do in my curve-hugging maroon halter mini dress. But still.

"I … damn. I'm sorry, Becca," Jules finally says. "What can I do?"

"Thanks. But I'm good. Really. This is huge, you guys coming out with me like this. I miss you both so much. So let's just get in there, do our thing, and have a blast."

She nods. "Roger that."

"How about you?" I nudge. "I know this isn't the best time of year. Need some help finding a little stress release in there?" I give her a knowing smile. Jules is so all about her job that I've never even known her to date, much less hook up in a club. But it's worth a shot.

"Oh, please, I'm sure everyone in there is at least ten years younger than me," she scoffs.

I laugh. "So? Plenty of young'uns likes them a cougar," I tease.

Jules wrinkles her nose and Sasha actually laughs.

"Thanks, but we'll leave that sort of 'stress release' to you," she responds drily.

I shrug just as we reach the entrance. "Suit yourself. But I'm still gonna get you drunk, happy, and dancing, girl," I promise.

"Now *that* I can handle," Jules replies with a giggle.

I lead her by the hand and, as soon as we're inside, the first thing we do is get drinks at the bar and sip them at a standing table, scoping out the dance floor. There are certainly plenty of hotties in the crowd, but one particular guy catches my eye immediately. With dark hair and big muscles, he looks a lot like Vincent, though not nearly as gorgeous. Still, could be fun.

I tap Sasha's shoulder and point the guy out. She rolls her eyes and gestures for me to lead the way, tugging at Jules to join us. Not to seem too eager, I start us at the opposite end of the floor. I dance with my girls, letting the music do its work and unwind the tension in my limbs.

I slowly work us across the room as the songs shift. But I lose track of the dude at some point. Oh, well. Sweaty and thirsty, at the next shift between songs, I haul Sasha and Jules back to the bar so we can get another drink and regroup.

"So what'd your man think of you coming out with us?" I ask Sasha loudly in her ear.

She rolls her eyes and yells back, "He told me if I came home horny to feel free to wake him up."

Jules laughs, but I give Sasha a worried look.

"You guys aren't already living together, are you?" I shout back.

She shakes her head violently. "No. He said he'd come over if I was. He's at his own place. Yeesh. We're definitely not there yet."

Relieved that my best friend isn't already at the cohabiting stage, which leads to the marriage stage, I down the rest of my drink. Not long later, I spot the guy again, and he's much closer this time. I gesture for them to follow, and we slink up close to him and his friends, dancing seductively with each other. Both Jules and Sasha seem to be enjoying themselves. We clearly all needed this. And I'm glad they're both here so they have each other, and I won't feel bad when I make my next move.

I turn around so my back is against Sasha's front, and I make eye contact with my target. He's tall. Much taller than Vincent. And he's not as good-looking as I thought he was from afar. Definitely a Monet. But I have just enough alcohol buzzing through my veins to not give a shit. So when he slides up, I give him a sultry look and let him gather me into his arms.

Monet spins me around so he's basically dry humping my ass, and I'm not exactly feeling anything that would impress me. I look up to see Sasha and Jules tolerating dancing with his friends. It makes me chuckle, and I hope at least Jules leans into it a little. Girlfriend could use a good roll in the hay with a younger man.

But then I notice the guy dancing with Sasha getting a little handsy. Reflexively, I pull her toward me protectively, stepping out of Monet's embrace. Sasha signals that she's okay, and Jules pulls in tighter. But Monet must not have liked me stepping away, because he persistently steps back up behind me, this time running his hands down my sides.

A shiver runs down my spine. I can't deny that being touched like that feels damn good. So I turn back around, and I don't resist when Monet bends down and tells me his name, which I forget practically instantly. I tell him my chosen fake club-hookup name, and mere moments later, we're making out. There's nothing special about it, though he's still more skilled than Quin. Not so skilled as Vincent. I crush that thought as soon as it crops up.

Or, I try to. Unfortunately I have to admit to myself that despite the initial thrill of being touched so sensually, kissing this guy feels like kissing a wall. Zero chemistry. Nothing like the sparks that I felt with Vincent. The fire. The toe-curling need to take it further. My stomach turns when I realize that if it weren't for Vincent, I'd be going home with this guy tonight and probably having a pretty good time. The motherfucker has ruined me.

I'm so angry, I press away, making an excuse about needing to use the ladies room. Sasha and Jules follow, and we tumble into the large, multi-stall room, sweaty and panting. Once the door closes, things are quiet enough for me to think. And quiet enough for them to ask questions.

"You okay?" Jules asks softly as we wait for our turns.

"Yeah, I'm fine," I say shortly.

"You don't sound fine," Sasha points out.

That gets a laugh out of me. "Yeah, okay, I'm not so fine right now. But I will be. I just don't want to dance with that guy anymore, that's all."

Jules and Sasha exchange a look. Thankfully, a stall opens up, giving me a moment to do my business and collect myself.

When we leave the ladies room, we go back

to our initial drink and dance mode, sticking with each other the rest of the night. It's fun, really. Much needed blowing off of steam. But not everything I was hoping it would be. No thanks to Vincent fucking DeMarco.

I SPEND THE REST OF THE WEEKEND contemplating this new reality where a man who drives me crazy is, ironically, the only one I can think of when I want to be driven crazy. Sexually, that is. It's pretty frustrating. It's interrupting my usual flow of dating around, having fun, then going on my way. But now?

Now I want a guy who sends me over the edge with one hungry look. A guy who I don't want to figure out but need to. I want Vincent. The maddening motherfucker.

"EXAM THREE IS READY FOR YOU. VITALS ARE entered, blood is drawn, and he's got his stool sample collection kit and instructions." I hand Sasha the folder in my hand.

"What's he here for?" She asks.

"He's got hypertension two with new symptoms. Tinnitus-like ringing in the ears and blood in his stool, thus the sample."

She frowns, looking through his history. "Did you go over his meds? He doesn't have antiplatelets listed, which those are both potential side effects of."

"I … did not go over that with him. Sorry," I reply with a grimace.

Sasha looks up with concern in her eyes. "You've been really off your game the last two days. You want to talk about it?"

"Later," I promise. "You should get in there. He's a crotchety old fucker."

She gives me a vague smile. "Right. Well, if you weren't my best friend I'd remind you not to talk about patients like that. But since you are, I'll point out I have class tonight. I'm free tomorrow, though."

"Tomorrow night, then," I assure her, plastering on a convincing smile.

"Okay." She reaches out and squeezes my shoulder.

I try harder to pretend like my head is in the game.

It works until Harper finds me that afternoon.

"Hey," she greets me, looking just as chipper as regular orgasms will make a girl.

I shake my head at my inner dialogue. I have got to do something before this bitterness eats me alive.

"Hey, girl, what's shakin'?"

"I wanted to invite you to a party this weekend. At Mason's place."

A host of thoughts and emotions flip through my mind. It must make me look like a fucking idiot, because Harper waves a hand in front of my face.

"Hello? You still in there?"

I shake myself, snapping my eyes back to hers. "Absolutely. Sorry. A party sounds like exactly what I need, thanks. Just let me know when and where, and I'll be there."

7

___

When I met up with Sasha on Wednesday night, I didn't breathe a word of what I had planned, because I knew she wouldn't approve. So here I am, at ten o'clock on Saturday night, headed to the party solo. With Sasha good and distracted by her man. If my plan fails, she needn't be any wiser. And I won't need to embarrass myself any more than necessary.

Because if Vincent is here, I'm going after what I want. And if he's not, I'm going to do what I have to do to move on.

Job one was to dress for success. If the hot pink mini halter dress I'm wearing doesn't do the trick, I don't know what will. My hair is on-point, carefully styled so my curls look glamorously messy. Most people don't get how much fucking work that is, but it's worth it. I look hot. Which will help with job two: Make him beg for it.

Here goes nothing.

I step out of the car and make my way up the walkway to the house Mason apparently shares with a few other guys. As I knock, I can hear music, and people, but none of it sounds out of control. Hopefully, this won't be boring.

When nobody answers after a minute, I try the handle. It opens immediately. The small entryway holds a few people I don't recognize who don't even look up as I walk in. There's a kitchen to my right with a bunch of dudes tapping a keg. With a roll of the eyes, I keep going, hoping this isn't some college-level kegger. Just down the hall, the space opens to a large living room where music plays and people holding drinks talk in small groups all over the room.

"Becks," I hear just as I spot Harper with a small group of girls. She rushes over and hugs me. "I'm so glad you're here. Come meet some of Mason's college buddies."

"Um, sure, yeah, okay," I agree, allowing her to pull me along. She brings me over to the group she was in, and I notice Avery for the first time. "Hey, girl." I give her the nod, which she returns.

Harper introduces me to three other girls so quickly I know I'll never remember their names. Wendy? Natalie? Julie? I don't know. Doesn't really matter anyway, I'll probably never see them again.

They continue chatting about where they get their nails done or some shit like that, and I totally zone out, my eyes scanning the room for signs of Vincent. But nothing. I don't see Mason either.

"Where's your man?" I ask, tugging at Harper's elbow.

"He and some of the guys went to get more booze. They'll be back soon," she explains.

"Isn't there a keg in the kitchen? Or did I miss something?"

She laughs. "Yeah, but apparently they killed the last of the hard alcohol, so they went to get more," she says with a shrug.

"Ah. Well. I think I'll stick to beer tonight

anyway. Be back." I don't want to get too hammered. At least, not yet.

She nods, and I slip away from the group. I make it into the kitchen to find a few guys still hovering around the keg.

"What have we got, boys?" I ask coyly, slinking up next to the tallest. He's pretty hot too, with dark brown hair, green eyes, and a swimmer's bod.

He grins down at me, revealing a dimple on his left cheek. Hello, Plan B.

"Natty Ice," he replies. "Want some?"

I pluck a red cup from the stack on the counter. "Don't mind if I do," I reply, dispensing some of the cheap beer into the side of the cup. I still end up with a shit ton of foam. I take a gulp before extending my hand. "I'm Becca."

"I'm Sebastian. But you can call me Seb," he replies, taking my hand and squeezing.

"Nice to meet you, Seb," I reply. "How do you know Mason?"

"I don't. I'm here with Jay —" he points to the blond guy leaning against the sink "— who went to school with him."

I nod at Jay, saluting him with my cup before

taking another drink. I hear the front door open and a chorus of voices ring down the hall.

"We come bearing liquor," Mason's voice booms before the man himself appears in the already-crowded kitchen, forcing me to take a step closer to Seb. Who doesn't seem to mind at all based on the dimpled smile he shoots me as our hands brush together.

Mason sets down several bottles of cheap vodka just as Vincent appears in the doorway holding two Black Label bottles.

"Well, looks like someone splurged on the good stuff," I say, taking another sip of beer. Vincent's eyes meet mine before they flick to Seb standing next to me. But he doesn't say a word. He simply sets the bottles down, gets himself a glass from the cupboard, opens the bottle, and proceeds to pour himself a good three fingers of scotch before silently heading to the living room.

I smile secretly to myself. He seemed irritated. Hopefully by me, because getting under his skin is the first step.

I shoot the shit with Seb for a while, solidifying my options for later. Turns out he's a little younger than me, but he seems cool. He lifeguards for a gym chain. So I was right about the bod. That's definitely promising. But as he and the guys start talking about basketball, I quickly lose interest and head back into the living room.

Someone has turned the music up, and couples now litter the couches, some making out, some clearly on their way to making out. Great. I hope this isn't going to be one of *those* parties. Although … maybe I should hope for that, since all of my designs are along those lines anyway. But I don't want it to devolve into that before I've had time to make my play.

At least, that's my thinking until I spot Vincent seated in an armchair in the corner. With motherfucking Avery on his lap.

And when she leans down to kiss him, something inside me breaks. Which makes me realize, it's so much worse than I thought. Because if it was just about sex, I'd be angry. But I'm not. I'm *hurt*. And that forces me to admit to myself that I want Vincent for more than just sex.

I don't even bother dissecting when that happened. The question is, what do I do now? My instinct is to march over there and bitch-slap Avery right off his lap. My second thought is to go get Seb and dry fuck him on the couch in retaliation. But my third thought wins.

I head back to the kitchen and pour myself a huge glass of scotch, downing it in one go.

"Whoa, slow down there," Seb says, coming over to ease me off the bottle as I start to pour another.

Abandoning the alcohol, I go on my toes and press my lips to his, desperate to erase Vincent from my mind. He pushes me away gently.

"Hey, I think you're great but …" He stares at me awkwardly.

Nonononono. This is not happening.

Just then Vincent appears in the kitchen doorway again, his eyes landing on Seb with his hands holding my upper arms, our faces inches apart. He grabs the whole bottle of scotch and disappears with it without a word.

And in an instant, I'm furiously ripping away from Seb and following after Vincent.

"I wasn't done with that," I call angrily after him.

I burst into the living room, but he's nowhere to be seen. Except Avery is, seated in the armchair she'd been straddling him in. Kissing him in.

I'm standing in front of her before I even knew my feet were taking me there.

"Why'd you do it, bitch?"

Avery stands up to face me. "Do what?" Oh, she sounds innocent. But the small, triumphant smile on her face says otherwise.

"You kissed him. You went after him even though you knew —" I choke on the words for a moment. "You knew how much I liked him. All those weeks when we thought he had a girl-friend. You knew because you were the first one to try to bribe me with the truth."

Avery folds her arms over her chest, looking beyond smug. And it's all I can do not to punch her.

`"Guess he'd rather go for someone a little less crazy," she replies, her gaze shifting over my shoulder.

I glance back to find everyone watching. *Everyone*. Including him.

I turn back to her, my eyes searching hers for the friend I once thought I knew better. But Lacey, the maniacal bitch who once fucked with Sasha's life, was too close to Avery for too long. And I see more of Lacey in her now that her mask is off.

I sigh heavily and her smirk deepens.

I shake my head. "You shouldn't have fucked with me, Avery. Just remember what happened to Lacey." I back up slowly, refusing to turn my back to her. And for once, she has enough sense to look nervous.

I shoot daggers at Vincent as I walk by him. Maybe I knew him even less than I thought if he'd actually go for someone like her. Seb hovers in the hall just outside of the living room, clearly having witnessed the whole thing.

"Hey," he says, gently catching my arm. "Come with me?"

I look up into his emerald eyes and nod, letting him lead me out the door.

We settle on the porch, an awkward silence hanging between us.

Seb turns to me. "I don't know exactly what was going on back there, but I hope you're okay."

I huff a laugh. "I'll be all right. But thanks."

"I bet you will be. You seem pretty tough," he says. "I also wanted to let you know that I wasn't … when I said I came here with Jay. I meant *with* him." He looks at me meaningfully and it clicks.

"Oh my god," I gasp. I look back at the house, then lean in. "They don't know?"

He shakes his head, and I lay my hand over his.

"I won't say a word. Thank you for telling me, though."

"I figured you'd already had a rough enough night. I didn't want you to think I'd rejected you too."

"Well, you kind of did," I point out. "But at least for good reason. And hey, if you ever need a beard, I've totally got you."

Seb laughs. "I appreciate that, but I think it would *really* drive your boyfriend over the edge if you pretended to be with me, even if it was to keep my cover."

I blanch at his words. "He is most definitely not my boyfriend. Did you miss all of that in there?"

He looks at me knowingly. "I think I got the gist. You like him. Your friend made a move on him anyway. Did you miss how he was looking at you? Because I didn't."

He rises, extending a hand. I take it, letting him pull me up.

"He was looking at me?" I ask. And I hate how vulnerable it sounds.

"Yes. When he wasn't looking at me like he wanted to rip my head off for being near you. Trust me, whatever happened with that girl in there, he wasn't looking at her the way he looks at you."

"Nothing happened." Vincent's voice cuts sharply through our tête-à-tête.

I look back to see him hovering on the doorstep. As he moves toward us, Seb gives me a smile and slips around him, heading back into the house.

Vincent approaches, hands in pockets. "She kissed me. Apparently you saw that. Guess you didn't see me stopping her."

"Why was she on your lap in the first place? I thought you didn't even like her. At least that's what you —"

Vincent puts a finger on my lips.

"God, woman, do you ever stop talking?"

He pulls his hand away only to replace it with his mouth. There's none of the animalistic hunger of our first kiss. This is soft, yearning. As he sinks against me, wrapping his arms behind my back, pulling me into him, I return it and then some. I wind my fingers into his dark, luscious hair, pressing my body against his. He's right. I'm done talking. I'm done thinking. I'm done caring about who said or did what. I need him. I need this.

His hands dip to my backside, gently cupping me. He breaks the kiss and gives me that fiery look of his. "You're killing me with this dress."

I lick my lips and look up at him. "Then let's go somewhere you can take it off me."

I feel his cock twitch in his pants and he sucks in a breath, smoldering down at me.

"I don't know if that's such a good idea."

I pull away, my hands flying to my hips. "Excuse me?"

"I just mean …" He scrubs a hand through his hair. "God, I'm fucking this all up."

"Damn straight you are," I say, all sass. "You can't just drive-by-orgasm me, kiss me like you're tryin'a light a fire, then expect me to turn it all off on a dime." I go to push him sharply in the chest, but his hands close over my wrists before I can make contact. I gasp as he tugs me against him.

His eyes darken, his mouth set in a firm line

as he glares at me. One of his hands slips to my neck, his palm flat against my throat.

"I don't expect anything. And you shouldn't either."

Despite his words, his lips crash into mine, his hand slipping to the back of my neck to pull me in. The animal is back, and the urgency of his mouth on mine wipes all thought from my mind.

His hand snakes back around to the front of my neck as his mouth leaves mine. He tips my head up, using his tongue and teeth to tease my throat. I bow into him, more turned on than I can ever remember being.

I slip a hand down his back, over his ass, then between us to the hardness straining against his jeans.

"Please," I beg into his ear as he sucks at my shoulder.

He tears his mouth away in a flash and grabs my hand, pulling me urgently behind him into the house.

A few curious pairs of eyes follow us as we enter, then hook a sharp left down a hallway I haven't been in yet. Another turn at the end of the hall and we descend a short set of stairs into a sunken den. Vincent closes and locks the door at the top of the stairs behind us, plunging us into near darkness.

His mouth finds mine again, and the hunger is back. He pushes me to a sofa in the center of the room, toppling me onto the soft surface. I gasp and open my eyes. My sight has adjusted to the small bit of moonlight coming through a window in the corner. It highlights just enough of Vincent's face to see the desire written there.

He drops to his knees, placing himself between my legs. His hands skim up my thighs, pushing my dress up to my waist, exposing my thin, flesh-colored thong. He slides a finger under it, dipping between my folds, sucking in a breath at what he finds. His strong hands slide behind my bottom, pulling until I'm forced to lie back on the couch, my legs parted as he sinks his head between them.

With the hand he had between my legs, he pulls my thong to the side as his mouth opens to taste me. I throw my head back the instant I realize what he's about to do.

"Fuck, yes," I groan. So much for making him beg. But hell if I care right now.

And when his tongue masterfully parts me,

sliding mercilessly over every sensitive spot, I forget everything but the low ache building between my legs as he works. I was so wrong about him, about his skills, his priorities. Because based on the slow, pleasurable torment he's unleashing, the man is the exact opposite of all talk. It's the last thought I have before an orgasm takes me.

As I come down from the high, he raises himself over me, gathering my curls back from my face, kissing the side of my neck.

"That was fucking amazing," I moan into his ear. I feel him smile against my neck before he places a gentle kiss there. "But god, I can't wait to fuck you."

He pulls back to look at me, his expression inscrutable.

I run a finger down his cheek, deciding I'd rather not do this on the couch owned by a houseful of dudes. Who knows what's gone on here? And frankly, I'd like to take my time with the gorgeous man straddling me right now anyway.

"Do you want to come back to my place?" I ask in a sultry voice.

He closes his eyes and presses my whole

hand to his cheek before turning to place a kiss on my palm.

"I —"

Whatever Vincent was about to say is cut off by a loud banging on the door.

"Vincent? Becca? You in there?" Harper calls through the door. She sounds panicked. Panicked enough that Vincent jumps up. I follow, hastily fixing my dress as we scramble to the door.

Vincent unlocks it and throws it open to a worried-looking Harper. And behind her stands a police officer.

8

"Need to see some ID," the officer barks shortly.

Without a word, Vincent fishes his wallet out of his back pocket, retrieves his ID, and hands it over as I scramble for the zippered pocket on the side of my dress to get mine.

"What's this about, officer?" Vincent asks calmly.

With my ID in hand, I look up at the cop, whose eyes are now flicking between Vincent's license and his face. After a few more seconds of examining it, he hands it back over, gesturing for mine. I give it to him nervously.

He's silent as his eyes do the same dance

between the piece of plastic in his hand and me. Once he seems satisfied, he hands it back.

"Neighbors reported underage drinking," he finally tells Vincent. His gaze searches the room behind us, then back to Harper. "That everyone, ma'am?"

Harper nods vigorously, shooting us an apologetic look. The officer retreats back down the hall, and Vincent follows Harper, who follows the cop. So I'm not left with much choice.

As we walk, I see the officer tap on partially open doors, quickly scanning each room. When we reenter the main area, another officer is talking to Mason just off the entryway. The officer looks up to see his partner and finishes up with Mason, gesturing for the other cop to follow him. They both leave the house and the few people left are completely silent. The music has been turned off as well, and the whole place is eerily quiet.

Mason shoots a worried glance at Vincent.

"You okay, man?" he asks. "I wanted to warn you, since … you know. But I couldn't."

Vincent shoots him a death glare. "I'm *fine*," he snips tersely.

I give Harper a questioning look, and she just shrugs her shoulders.

"So what the hell was that all about?" I ask Mason, referring to the cops showing up.

Mason is still giving Vincent a concerned look, but his eyes move to me after a moment.

"The seventeen-year-old next door thought it would be a good idea to come over here after his parents were in bed and sneak some alcohol. I caught the kid drinking a beer in the kitchen and made him go home. Guess his parents found out anyway and called the cops."

I gasp. "Holy shit! You didn't get in trouble, did you?" I ask.

"Nah, they went and talked to the kid, and he finally admitted we didn't give him the booze, he just took it," Mason assures me. "But ya know, they still checked everyone's IDs anyway. Pretty much scared them all off. Guess the party's over."

As if to prove his point, the last few people left in the living room give him a wave and head out.

"You guys are welcome to stay, hang out, crash here or whatever if you don't wanna drive home," Mason offers, winding his arm around Harper's waist.

Harper looks at Vincent, then me, with a barely suppressed grin. Apparently, I'm not the only one who wants me to get laid tonight.

"Thanks, man, but I think I'm gonna head home," Vincent replies.

I can't help the incredulous look I give him. Really? He's not even going to talk to me first? I did just ask him to come to my place before the cops pretty much shat all over my plans to get some. Er, some more.

"Okay, man, I'll see you Monday," Mason replies, holding up a fist. They bump fists as Harper and I share a look. Boys are so fucking clueless.

"Well, I don't want to be a third wheel, so I guess I'll be going too," I say, trying not to let the sarcasm drip out of my voice as Vincent actually starts heading for the door. Damn.

"Hey, Vincent, you should walk Becca to her car," Harper pipes up. "You know, because it's late."

He turns back and gives me a questioning look.

"No need, I'm right out front," I say coolly, folding my arms over my chest. He wants to pull the hit-it-then-quit-it disappearing act again? Fine. Fool me once, shame on you. Fool me twice … well, fuck that shit.

"Suit yourself," he grunts, then leaves. Double damn. No, he didn't.

"Cool, well, thanks for coming. Sorry for the cops and stuff," Mason says to me. Seriously. Clueless.

"Yeah, no worries, dude," I assure him. "See you guys Monday."

"I'll walk you to the door," Harper mutters, slipping out of Mason's grip.

Mason looks like he's finally getting the clue that something just went down, because he turns and heads into the living room, looking puzzled but giving us plenty of space.

"I can't believe Vincent actually just left without you. Didn't you guys just …" Harper whispers questioningly when we get to the door.

I shake my head. "We didn't fuck, if that's what you're asking. Not that we were in there having a heart-to-heart or some shit either," I grumble.

"So what happened?" she presses.

I give her a skeptical look. Sure, I told Sasha about our first sexual encounter at the bar, but I didn't tell Harper. Don't get me wrong, she and I have had a lot of fun together, but neither of us can keep our mouths shut. And we work with the dude. I really don't want to deal with all that if I don't have to.

"Fine, don't tell me, then," she says with an exasperated sigh.

"I want to, I just … I guess I don't really know what happened. But he's all over the damn place, so I'm just going to go home and just try to forget about him," I admit.

She shakes her head and pulls me in for a hug. "I'm going to earn your trust back. I promise, okay?"

I squeeze her back with a laugh. "You do that, boo. But I'm still not telling."

She huffs a little laugh and presses me away. "See you Monday?"

"Unless I win the lottery," I joke. And with a smile, I slip out the front door.

Only to find Vincent on the other end of the wide front porch.

I cross my arms over my chest. "I said I can walk myself to my own damn car," I say.

He looks back at me. "I know you can. But you also asked if I wanted to go home with you."

"And you said you were going home. You know. Your home. Not mine," I point out.

He shrugs, turning toward me fully as I join him at the edge of the porch.

"Maybe I changed my mind," he replies.

I snort. There's a shocker. "Well, maybe I've changed mine too," I return.

He raises an eyebrow and runs a hand down my bare arm, eliciting traitor shivers down my spine. "You sure about that?" he asks lowly.

"Maybe I'll change it back if you tell me why Mason was worried about you and the cops," I reply.

Vincent's hand drops back to his side and he scowls. "There are things you don't want to know about me."

"You mean there are things you don't want me to know about you."

He shakes his head. "Same difference."

"No, there's a big difference," I disagree.

"It doesn't matter. Let's just go back to your place," he insists, stepping closer and looking down into my eyes with an intense gaze that, despite myself, sends heat ripping through me.

"Oh, *now* you want to fuck me?"

"Isn't that what you wanted?" he asks, confused.

"Yes. But I don't *just* want to fuck you, you dumbass," I grind out. "Don't ask me why, but for some insane reason I want more than that. Wanted more than that. Starting with the story on you and the cops. But now? You're being all weird again, and I'm starting to lose my patience with this bullshit."

"I've been pretty up front with you, Becca," he replies calmly. "I'm not looking for a girl-friend. But I like you. And I'm sick of trying not to fuck you."

"Well, that's romantic," I reply sarcastically.

He laughs. "If you want romance, you're really barking up the wrong tree," he says. His eyes still glittering with laughter, he looks down at me again. "But if you're looking for someone to worship every inch of your gorgeous fucking body, I can definitely help you with that."

My breath catches in my throat. Goddamn him. He drives me fucking crazy. But that's just it. I'm into this guy on so much more than a physical level. Don't get me wrong: I'm not the girl who thinks she can change a man. But damn do I want to understand him.

And he's wrong about the romance. Dancing with me like our bodies were made to fit together? Sitting with me in a dark alley so I'm not alone? Fixing my back after a stressful week? Giving me orgasms with no expectation of getting them back? He's not acting like a guy who isn't thinking about what would make me happy. Even if he keeps saying he's not. He's a pile of contradictions.

But he's also unfortunately done things to my body I'll never forget. Twice. Is that why I'm so into this guy?

I have to admit that the answer to that is, *Maybe*. Or maybe it's my ego; maybe I just want to conquer him. Either way, I for sure don't want him for just a good fuck, though at this point he's proven he would be. I'm just as stupid and stubborn as he is. We're either perfect for each other or we're sexual napalm, about to explode all over downtown San Diego.

"I have to think about it," I finally reply.

"Really?" he asks, his brows pulled together.

"Really," I reply, hands planted firmly on my hips.

He stares down at me, and I wonder if he's about to try to get me in bed anyway. I stare back up at him stubbornly. But inside, I'm quaking. I hope he doesn't see because I'm not sure I could resist. Or maybe I hope he does. Goddamn, I'm driving *myself* crazy.

"Okay," he says, taking a step back. "I'll walk you to your car."

I'm simultaneously relieved and disappointed. So what do I do? I start walking. He slips his large hand around mine and walks me the short distance to where I'm parked.

I reclaim my hand to take my car key out of my zipper pocket. When I look back up, I barely have time to brace myself as his face lowers to mine, his mouth closing gently over my lips in a soft, innocent kiss that makes me want to throw his fine ass in the car and drag him home for something much less innocent.

Thankfully, he pulls back after just a moment, saving me from myself.

"See you around, Becca," he says, stepping

back and giving a small wave. I watch as he wanders off down the road. But before he can turn around and catch me, I get in the damn car to go home and go to sleep. Alone. Again.

But I can't be mad at him. It's my own damn fault this time.

9

"**I**'m proud of you," Sasha says, carrying the salad bowl from the kitchen and putting it on her dining room table.

"I can't decide if I'm proud of me too or if I need to get my head examined," I mutter as I fill my plate.

She chuckles and settles into the seat across from me. "Well, he isn't exactly the kind of guy I'd have hoped you'd fall for, but it had to happen sometime," she replies.

"I'm not *falling for him*," I scoff, stabbing a tomato angrily. "And what's wrong with him?"

I hear a spluttering cough coming from the living room, and I roll my eyes.

"Is peanut gallery over there going to be here

the whole time, or what?" I ask, shooting a dirty look toward where Sasha's boyfriend is sitting.

"Sorry," she says with a shrug. "Like I said earlier, he's only here for the next few days while his place is being fumigated. But I've got to be honest, I'm kind of with him on this one. Are you sure you want to start something with this guy knowing it's never going to be what you really want?"

"Fine, have a point then," I say dramatically. "Of course I'm not sure. Thus the girl talk. Well … girl and Cal."

"Consider me one of the girls," he calls in his beautiful, deep British-accented voice.

Knowing he can't see me, I give a dramatic shiver for Sasha's benefit, and she laughs.

"Good thing Vincent doesn't have an accent like that, or we'd be having a very different conversation right now," I whisper to her before taking another bite.

"You have *no* idea," Sasha whispers back. "The dirty talk?" She shakes a hand up and down and rolls her eyes back in her head, demonstrating how hot it is.

"You're killing me," I groan. But I'm happy for her. She almost never talks about this kind of stuff, so he must be doing something right. Doing her right. A lot.

Cal appears behind Sasha. All more than six feet of his tanned, muscled, and stupidly hot self. Wearing a fitted T-shirt. Damn. He leans down and kisses her chastely on the side of her neck.

"I couldn't quite hear whatever you girls were just talking about, but my ears were burning," he teases as he straightens up.

I eye him openly as I continue to eat.

"I'd like to think my cooking is amazing, but I'm pretty sure that's not why you're drooling," Sasha says drily.

I snap my eyes back to hers with an innocent smile and a shrug.

"He should dress like that at work," I suggest, waggling my eyebrows.

Cal smirks as he heads into the kitchen to refill his coffee cup.

"Like I don't know you all are staring at me already. No need to make *that* worse," he says crisply.

I have to laugh. "Drat! I've been caught," I joke.

"You're not exactly subtle about it, my

dear," Sasha points out.

"Well, we can't all date a Dr. Hottie. So sue me if I like to appreciate the goods."

Cal rolls his eyes as he takes a seat at the table between us.

"Maybe not, but please for the love of all that's good, don't settle," he replies, blowing on the hot liquid in his cup. "There's nothing less attractive than a woman who doesn't know her worth."

My eyebrows pull together. "I don't know if I should be flattered or insulted by that," I say honestly.

"My apologies," he says in his oh-so-British way. "Let me rephrase. You have a lot to offer, and you deserve better than the way he's been behaving. That's all."

"Oh," I say. "Well … thanks?" I give Sasha a bewildered look.

"I have to agree," she states. "But, unfortunately, you're already really into him. Do you think he's capable of more?"

I shake my head vehemently. "Nuh-uh. Not gonna go there. Whether he is or not, you know I don't play the 'fix him' game," I insist.

"Well, then, I think you have your answer," she says simply with a sorrowful look.

I sigh and finish my food. I both love and hate having friends who make me admit what's best for me. Because she's right, this is a recipe for bad. I'm not going to try to change him. He just wants sex and, strangely, for once I don't. So despite his *many* other attractive qualities, the fundamentals don't add up.

"I hope you guys are looking for a third wheel," I tell them both. "Because I'm going to need help staying out of trouble."

Sasha gives Cal a look, to which he nods.

"We've got your back, babe," she says firmly, laying a hand over mine and squeezing.

"You take Monday, Wednesday, and Friday," Cal says to Sasha. "I'll watch her on Tuesday and Thursday while you're in class."

I give him a look. "You don't have to fucking *babysit* me," I say with a sneer. "Oh, wait. Except on Friday. Happy hour. I *cannot* go to that, and I'm going to need someone to make sure I don't do anything stupid. So actually, yeah, there might be some babysitting required."

We all bust up laughing. Always better to laugh than cry, I say.

"I DON'T KNOW WHY I LET YOU MAKE ME WATCH this crap," Sasha groans, sinking into the couch.

"Mel Brooks is a fucking god," I reply defensively. "How can you not like *Young Frankenstein*?"

She shrugs and yawns.

"Oh, you did not just yawn while Dr. Frankenstein is meeting Frau Blücher," I chastise her.

Sasha delves deeper into the cushions, pulling a blanket over her as she lazily watches the screen. "Sorry, long week," she says on another yawn, then frowns deeply. "What's with the horses?"

I glance between her and the movie. "Damn, this comedy gold is lost on you, boo," I say, shaking my head. "Just go to sleep already." I sigh and lean back into the couch, pulling my knees up to my chest.

It's not long before Sasha is snoring softly beside me, so I lose myself in the movie, even though I've watched it about a thousand times and could probably act it out verbatim. But I guess that's why it's so comforting.

I've just finished watching the movie and am debating whether to move on to *Spaceballs* or just go to bed when there's a soft knock on the door. My brows pull together, knowing it's not Cal. Sasha and I were going to have a sleepover tonight to keep me strong, and I doubt he'd want to get all up in that. And lord knows Harper is probably all up in Mason right now. Or, you know, the other way around.

I slip silently off the couch and tiptoe toward the door. A glance out the peephole shows me a shock of dark hair and a leather jacket that instantly raises my hackles. I slip the chain off and open the door, my indignation purposely on full display.

"Vincent," I hiss, and his dark eyes snap up to meet mine. "What the fuck are you doing here?"

He runs a hand through his hair, his eyes tired. But he still looks like sex and sin. Bastard.

"I need to talk to you," he says, sounding as tired as he looks.

I slip out the front door, letting it rest against the frame behind me and folding my arms over my chest as I glare up at him. "Well, I don't need to talk to you," I whisper-hiss. "How do you even know where I live?"

"Harper," he says with a shrug, his voice low. "And why are we whispering?"

I roll my eyes. "Sasha's asleep on my couch," I reply, jerking my head back toward the inside of the apartment. "And I'm going to fucking kill Harper."

"Don't — I snatched your info off her phone when she wasn't paying attention. She really needs to use a passcode," he says. "So can we go inside and talk, or what? I'd really rather not do this out here."

I raise my eyebrows. "I'm sorry, was I talking to myself a second ago? I've got nothing to say to you," I reiterate.

He raises an eyebrow in return. "What happened to thinking about it?" he asks.

"Oh, I thought about it," I assure him. "Not interested."

A smirk settles on his gorgeous lips. "Yeah, well, as much as I doubt that that's really true, I've been doing some thinking too," he says.

I scoff a laugh. "I hope you didn't hurt yourself," I reply.

"Mmm, see, that right there," he says, taking

a step toward me with a glint in his eye that's half smolder, half warning. "You wouldn't be angry if you didn't feel anything."

He stops inches shy of me, and I instinctively pull away. But my back hits the doorframe. And there's nowhere to go as he stares intently down at me.

"I didn't say I didn't feel anything. I said I'm not interested in doing anything about it," I insist. But my voice sounds small and unsure. I try to tell myself it's just the physical effect being so close to him has on me. But staring up into his eyes has a way of stripping me bare. The rawness in his gaze is impossible to hide from.

"Not even if I'm willing to meet you halfway?" he asks softly, his breath hot on my face.

In spite of myself, I'm intrigued. "I thought you weren't looking for a girlfriend?"

A half smile pulls at his lips. "I'm not. And I don't know ..." He looks up at the ceiling. "I'm not promising anything." His eyes flick back down to mine. "But when you walked away last Saturday, it didn't take me long to admit to myself that I didn't just want to fuck you either."

His admission takes the breath right out of me, and all I can do is blink up at him stupidly for a minute. No sassy comeback. No challenging questions. I'm struck dumb.

"What, exactly, are you proposing?" I finally manage to ask.

His broad shoulders lift gently. "I'll answer your questions, if I can. You decide if you still want to take it to the next level," he says simply.

"And what about you? Do you get to ask me questions to decide if that's what you want too?" I shoot back.

Vincent's eyes go hard, and I suck in a breath.

"I said I'm not looking for a girlfriend. Not that I didn't want one."

I stare up at him, totally baffled. Well, that's confusing as fuck. It takes my brain a minute to unravel that and realize … maybe he actually does want me in the same way. But … can't? And now I have a *million* questions.

"Okay," I agree abruptly. "I get to ask you questions. As long as you're going to answer them honestly."

"If I can," he repeats.

My eyes narrow. "Is that douchebag for, 'I'm going to do whatever it takes to get in your pants'?" I ask skeptically.

Vincent tips his head back and laughs. "If that was my plan, wouldn't I have done that last Saturday?" he asks.

"You really think you could've?" I challenge him, tightening my arms over my chest as I glare up at him resolutely.

He smirks down at me. "I think we both know the answer to that," he says with a slow shake of his head. "Look, we can take sex off the table completely if it makes you feel better."

"Why the hell would that make me feel better?" I reply. "I want to fuck you, dipshit — I just want you to let me in a little first."

"So, is that a yes?" he asks with a small smile.

"It's not a no," I say with a sigh, still not sure if all this is worth it.

I feel a burst of air on my back and spin around to see the door now wide open, with Sasha standing behind me looking tired and cranky.

"I see we have company," she says pointedly, her eyes meeting mine before turning a hostile glare on Vincent.

"I was just stopping by to say hi to Becca," Vincent replies. "But it's late, and I should let you guys get back to … whatever it was you were doing."

"Say hi?" Sasha scoffs, in total protector mode. "If you just wanted to say hi you wouldn't have showed up this late on a Friday night." Her unspoken implication hangs in the air.

I turn back to Vincent with a smirk. "Girl's got a point," I agree.

"I swear, all I wanted to do was talk," he replies, holding up his hands.

Sasha grabs me by the arm, pulling me back inside with a roll of her eyes. "That's what they all say," she grumbles.

"Wait," he says, throwing up a hand to keep her from closing the door. "What do you say, Becca? Give me a chance?"

Sasha looks at me questioningly.

"He wants to answer my questions," I explain to her. "See if I still want to go out with him after that."

Sasha's eyes narrow as she takes Vincent in.

"You need to ask at least twenty-four hours in advance. And it has to be during daylight hours, *in public*," she insists.

"Boy, your mom is really strict," Vincent

jokes with a sparkle in his eye, causing Sasha to shoot him a death glare. "Fine. Becca, can I please take you to lunch on Sunday, *in public*, so we can talk?"

Sasha looks at me impatiently, and I sense she wants me to tell him to fuck off. Which I'm not going to do. But it also seems, shall we say, imprudent to just cave.

I tap a finger to my chin in an obviously theatrical demonstration of thought.

"Hmmm, I just don't know," I murmur. "How about I check my social calendar and let you know tomorrow?"

A knowing smile pulls at Vincent's mouth. "You do that," he says with a chuckle. "Goodnight, ladies." And with a wink, he leaves.

Sasha can't close the door fast enough.

"I swear, I'm asleep for a minute and you —"

"Nuhnununuh," I protest, interrupting her. "You were asleep for a couple hours, boo, and you're not putting this one on me. I didn't ask him to come over here. My mind was made *up*."

"And now?" she presses, settling back onto the couch and pulling the blanket over her.

I shrug. "Couldn't hurt to see what he has to say."

She huffs a sarcastic laugh. "Oh, yes, it could. That one has trouble written all over him."

"And you think his friends aren't saying that about me?" I point out.

Sasha laughs. "Fair enough."

I pick up a throw pillow and whack her with it. "Well, damn, girl, you weren't supposed to agree with me," I tease.

"The truth hurts," she jokes back, pulling the pillow from behind her and fighting back.

We go at each other playfully for a few minutes before she freezes and drops her pillow.

"What?" I ask, worried at the stricken look on her face.

"Oh my god, this is exactly what guys think girls do at sleepovers," she says in horror, looking down at the pillows in our laps.

I burst out laughing. "Careful, or I'm gonna ask your fine-ass man to come over here and take a video of us doing it," I tease.

She pulls a grossed-out face. "Oh, gross, Becks, too far," she protests.

I cackle with delight. "Sasha, my darling

bestie," I say with a sigh. "You know I live to take it too far."

"Yes, I do know," she says, pulling a face. "I'd warn you to keep a lid on that on Sunday, but I know I'd be wasting my breath."

I pull my head back. "We'll see. If you didn't notice, I haven't agreed to anything yet."

"*Yet*," she stresses. "But let's be honest. You're going for it. You don't know how to *not* go for it, Becca."

I chew on my lip. "Yeah, you're right about that," I agree. "Am I crazy?"

"Absolutely," she says with a smile. "But it's one of my favorite things about you. You've talked me out of my comfort zone more times than I can count. And it was almost always a good thing."

"It's *always* a good thing," I correct her. "Even when shit goes bad. Because that's life, boo. We gotta take our lumps and learn from them."

"Well, for what it's worth, I hope Vincent's not a lump," Sasha offers.

I give her a distracted smile. "Me too, babe. Me too."

10

"I have to admit, I'm a little surprised you didn't pick the Italian restaurant."

Vincent shrugs as he sits across the secluded booth in the tiny, hole-in-the-wall taco place he picked in the heart of downtown.

"It's so close to my place that I already eat there too much anyway," he replies before taking a bite of the last of his carne asada fries. "And I like the food here."

I set my napkin down, my plate now completely empty of the amazing chicken burrito that had sat there a few minutes ago.

"Well, that was the best burrito I've ever

had," I admit. "How'd you find this place?" I reach for my water glass.

He wipes his mouth with a napkin, sets it down, then points at the north wall.

"Do you know what's a block away?" he asks cryptically.

Mystified, I shake my head.

"It's the San Diego County Jail, Becca. I got out of jail one night, and I was hungry. That's how I found this place."

It's hard to render me speechless, but the man seems to have a talent for it. I sit there in silence, while he patiently stares back at me with his dark, soulful eyes. For someone who doesn't talk much, his eyes sure say a lot. Right now they're begging me to say something, but I don't know where to even start with that.

And suddenly it hits me.

"That's what Mason meant about the cops. That's why you thought I'd decide I wasn't interested after all," I say, comprehension settling over me.

"Yes," he admits, leaning back with a sigh.

"So what'd you do?" I ask as casually as I can.

He smirks at me, his hand ruffling his dark hair. "I didn't do anything."

I roll my eyes. "Fine. What were you arrested for doing?"

He leans forward onto his arms. "My boss at the time accused me of stealing equipment from him."

"Is that why you work at the hospital now?"

Vincent blinks. "That was about ten steps ahead of the conversation I pictured happening in my head," he replies.

I laugh. "Sorry, my brain jumps around sometimes," I respond with a shrug.

He blows out a breath. "It's cool. But yeah. The stuff he accused me of stealing was magically found in my truck, so the charges stuck. Luckily, I didn't have to do any more time, just got slapped with a fine and a hefty parole since he got all his shit back and it was a first offense. My parole officer got me a job at the hospital. Good thing, since it's not exactly easy to find work with a record."

"You'd seriously never been arrested before?" I ask curiously.

He laughs. "That's what you want to know?"

I shrug.

He shakes his head.

"Yeah, I'd been arrested before. But not for anything serious. Underage drinking, criminal mischief, that sort of thing, years ago when I was just a kid, though that was back in Queens. Grand larceny is a whole other level."

"Wow," I murmur, tracing my finger over the design in the tablecloth.

"So any of this freaking you out?" he asks.

My eyes flick back up to meet his. "Do you want it to?" I challenge.

His answering smile knocks me on my ass. "No," he admits. "No, I don't."

"Is that why you can't have a girlfriend? Because you're on parole?" I ask, hoping I don't sound stupid. As blasé as I've been about my dating life, I've never dated someone who has been on parole, or even in jail, for that matter. Though one of my older brothers has been arrested a few times for things similar to Vincent's youthful indiscretions — except as an adult.

"Something like that," he replies slowly.

"How much longer?"

"Six months."

I pull nervously at my napkin, tearing it into pieces.

"That's not so bad," I reply.

"Not by itself. But it's just the beginning. Things aren't going to be easy, even after that," he responds.

I look up into his eyes. "I'm sorry," I tell him honestly. "Is there any way to appeal? To prove you didn't do it and clear the record?"

He shrugs. "Maybe, but that would take a lawyer I don't have money for, among other things."

"So, what, you just planned on never having a girlfriend because your life is too complicated? On just having casual sex for the rest of your life?" I ask.

He laughs. "I hadn't planned on anything." He pauses, his eyes darkening. "Especially not you."

That gets a small smile out of me. "I hadn't planned on you either. I've never exactly been the girlfriend type, anyway. So maybe we just keep talking, see how things go," I suggest as carefully and casually as I can. Not wanting to admit that this guy makes me feel things that defy logic.

Vincent appraises me silently while rubbing his cheek.

"I've never been great at taking things slow," he finally says.

"Me neither," I admit with a grin. "But then, it's been a really long time since I've wanted to take things anywhere. So maybe that's worth not fucking up."

His eyes cloud over as he studies my face. "I agree, but that's kind of the problem," he replies slowly.

I tilt my head and raise an eyebrow. "How's that?"

He looks down into his hands, the first self-conscious thing I think I've ever seen him do.

"Because my life is already fucked up. And I'm afraid bringing you into it is just going to end in disappointment," he replies honestly. His eyes drift slowly up to meet mine. "But I can't stop thinking about you."

I close my eyes at his words, a surge of heat rushing into my cheeks, my chest, and … other places.

I open my eyes once the sensation has passed. "I'm a big girl, I think I can handle it," I assure him. "And it's not exactly like I'm all sunshine and roses. I think you're getting into just as much shit as I am."

It's meant as a joke but also as a warning. I don't really know how to do relationships. Sure, my parents have been together forever, but they fight as much as they fuck. Which is a lot. Not really what I want out of life. But what *do* I want? I don't really know. Right now … him. And that's about as far as I've thought. I want Vincent DeMarco. All of him.

Sasha's going to kill me.

"What about work? You don't think it'll be weird?" he asks.

I snort. "Well, first of all, it's not like it's anybody's business anyway. Second, Mason and Harper seem to be handling it just fine. So even if people do find out, it's not the end of the world," I reply. Though I'm not exactly looking forward to the rumor mill knowing my business.

"So, we're doing this?" he asks softly.

I shrug. "Looks like. Strap in, it's going to be a hell of a ride."

A smile cuts across his handsome face and he rises, extending his hand. I take it, and we leave the restaurant, walking around downtown for a while.

We window shop, make small talk, and try out the whole getting-to-know-each-other thing. Did I mention all while holding hands? The sweetness and simplicity of it is mind-bogglingly emotional for me. It's *intimate*, and scary for me in a way casual sex isn't. Ironic, really — normalcy is terrifying to me. It almost makes me laugh that he thinks he's the one with the baggage. This guy has no idea what he's gotten himself into.

When he walks me back to my car later that afternoon, we step into our first awkward moment since lunch. He stares at me, clearly unsure whether he should make a move.

But this time, I know what to do. I've been fighting against my usual way of doing things all afternoon, but not now. With a grin, I step into him, going on my toes to press my lips to his.

He hesitates for only a moment before wrapping his arms around me and pulling me into him, opening his mouth against mine, running his tongue along my lip.

A shudder rolls through me, and I lace my fingers into his hair, deepening the kiss by meeting his tongue with mine. Knowing what he can do with that amazing fucking tongue makes keeping control incredibly difficult.

But after a minute, I pull back, determined to play by the rules. He looks down at me, desire clear in his eyes.

"That's not going to help me take things slow," he says in a husky voice.

"I'm sorry, did you not want me to kiss you? Because next time I —"

I'm cut off when his mouth descends on mine hungrily, his body pressing me into the side of my car. His hot mouth consumes mine, his hands skating down my neck, shoulders, and sides. The light touch of his fingers is a stark contrast to the heavy insistence of his lips, his tongue, and the whole thing has me melting into him, humming with need.

When he finally breaks away, I'm so worked up that "going slow" isn't even in my vocabulary anymore.

"I'll see you on Wednesday?" he asks, smirking down at me.

I look up at him, still trying to control my breathing. He looks so fucking smug, I realize he just did that on purpose. Got me all worked up on purpose.

"Did you just revenge turn me on?" I demand.

A look of pure and complete innocence settles over his face. It looks totally out of place on him. He may have the most gorgeous face in God's creation, but he's as far from angelic as it gets.

"I have no idea what you're talking about," he replies, fooling nobody.

"You're playing with fire," I warn him, ignoring his denial.

The smile drops off of his face, and he places his hands on my cheeks. "I know," he says softly, kissing my lips gently, chastely. "Wednesday." He drops his hands and waits for my agreement. The quiet smolder in his eyes makes my insides clench.

I swallow hard and nod. We're both playing with fire. And fuck if I don't want to burn with him.

***

WEDNESDAY NIGHT IS SPENT IN A SIMILAR fashion, going out to dinner after work and wandering around yet another part of San Diego

I'm not very familiar with. We end up in a small bar with a live band. It means I get to dance with him, but since the music is upbeat, it's not the suggestive, sensual kind I'd like it to be.

Still, his strong body moving against me is never a bad thing. And the more time we spend together, the more we find we're alike. It's funny, really, since outwardly we have such different personalities, and he was raised on the East Coast, an only child of a single father. A far cry from vying for attention with four older brothers and two questionably sane parents. And lord knows I'm a Cali girl, through and through.

But we like so many of the same things, have similar outlooks on life, and then there's the whole deep, intense physical attraction. That part's only getting stronger by the minute. Though it still feels like he's holding back on some level.

When we part that night with another epically delicious and frustrating make-out session at my car with a promise to see each other at the usual team happy hour on Friday, I start to question exactly how slow I'm really capable of going.

"So, am I actually going to get to spend time with you this evening, or is Vincent going to be stealing your attention again?" Sasha asks impatiently on Friday afternoon as we input patient file data.

"He'll be there, but Jules is finally done with all that budget shit and is going to join us. So while we're at the bar, I'll be all about my girls, I promise," I assure her.

She heaves a big sigh. "I'm starting to understand how you must've felt when Cal and I started dating," she replies drily.

I bat my eyelashes at her. "Nah, that's different. I had other friends to hang out with," I reply with a wink. Though I'm kind of lying. I did notice, and it did sting a little to lose my best friend, especially since I didn't know that's what she was doing at the time. But water under the bridge, and I'm not going to make her feel bad about disappearing or hiding it from me.

"Hey, I have other friends," she protests.

I smirk at her. "Besides Jules?"

She shoots me a dirty look but can't refute the truth of it. I give her a big smile back.

"Fine, you and Jules are my only friends. Happy?" she asks with a pout.

"Meh," I reply flippantly. *I'd be a lot happier if I was getting a piece of Vincent's fine ass right now*, I think to myself.

Sasha gives me a look like she knows what I'm not saying.

"So you've been uncharacteristically quiet about the whole Vincent thing," Sasha points out. "Everything going okay?"

I shrug. "We're taking it slow," I admit, trying not to show how impatient I am with even the idea of it.

Sasha barks a laugh. "Well, that's a first," she says.

I look at her, ready to play it down, but something inside me breaks.

"It's toooooooortuuuuuure," I whine. "I just want to jump his damn bones. But I don't want to scare him off either. Gahhhh, Sasha, I don't know what to dooooo." I slump my head forward onto the desk dramatically.

Sasha rubs my back in gentle circles. "Okay, I have to ask. Why would jumping his bones scare him off?" she asks quietly.

I force myself upright and give her an exhausted look. "Because I like him, Sasha," I admit. "I *really* like him. Like … want to crawl-inside-him-and-let-my-universe-go-quiet kind of like him."

Her eyes widen. "Okay, not exactly how I'd used that phrase, but … holy shit, Becks," she breathes. "That's … wow. Yeah, I could see how that would scare him off."

I frown, letting my brow dip exaggeratedly. "Would you stop agreeing with me already? It's fucking annoying," I snipe, half-joking.

"Sorry," she replies with a shrug. "But maybe it's better if he knows how you feel. Because if he can't handle that now, I don't think that's going to change with time. You guys are either on the same page, or you're not."

"That's a little more truth than I can handle right now," I grumble.

"Well thank fuck that I can give that back to you for once," Sasha teases.

I shoot her a dirty look. "Is that really what I'm like?"

"God, yes," she agrees emphatically. "Irritating, isn't it?" She smiles beatifically, and I have to laugh.

"Honestly? Yes. Very. God bless you for putting up with me."

She lays a hand over mine. "All joking aside, you're an awesome friend, Becca, and as hard as it is to hear the truth sometimes, I know I can always count on you for it. And if Vincent doesn't see how amazing you are and jump all over that, then he's an idiot who doesn't deserve you."

My eyes fill with tears, and I throw my arms around my best friend.

"Thanks, boo, that's exactly what I needed to hear right now."

She squeezes me back reassuringly.

"Good. Now get back to work so we can finish up and get our drink on," she commands, pulling away.

I give her a look. "Boy, I'm really starting to rub off on you, aren't I?" I tease.

She gives me a wink. "You wish."

I can't help but burst out laughing. "Okay, who are you, and what have you done with my best friend?" I ask between gales of laughter. Then I shake my hands. "No, no, no. Never mind. I take it back. I like this Sasha. She's *extra*."

She grins but blushes a little, so I know my Sasha is still in there. Though I also can't help noticing how fucking happy she looks. How free. And damn if that isn't how being in love should make you feel. The thought would bring me back down to earth if I wasn't so happy for her. So I focus on that.

"You did *not* tell MacDougall to go fuck himself in front of the entire budget committee," Sasha shrieks while laughing at Jules's confession.

"Well, I didn't use those exact words," Jules admits. "But pretty close." She grins.

"Oh my god, once that gets around, you're

going to be hero-worshipped," I tell her. Sasha and I exchange glances before throwing ourselves down toward Jules's side of the table in *Wayne's World*-esque supplication as we start chanting, "We're not worthy!"

Harper, who is on the other side of the booth, laughs uproariously, causing her to choke on the sip of beer she'd taken. I stop my adoration to clap her on the back.

"Easy there, tiger," I tease her.

She waves a hand and sniffs deeply, indicating that she's fine.

"So, Avery still too chicken to show her face?" I ask Harper, changing the subject.

She nods as she finishes wiping her nose. "She doesn't even talk to me anymore. I found out she's still hanging out with Lacey and read her the riot act. She won't so much as look at me now."

Sasha stiffens next to me. "No big loss if she's hanging out with Lacey," Sasha says frostily.

And that's as mean as my bestie ever gets. Because that bitch Lacey almost fucked up Sasha's career, her nurse practitioner degree, and her relationship with Cal.

Thankfully, we're saved any more awkwardness by the arrival of Ethan and Mark, who slide into the booth on Jules's side.

We exchange greetings, and I note that Mark is alone.

"Hey, where's Nina?" I ask him.

He exchanges an awkward look with Ethan.

"Yeah, uh, Nina and I aren't seeing each other anymore," he admits.

"Oh, bummer, I'm sorry to hear that," I reply.

He shrugs. "It's cool, but thanks." And that's all he says on the subject.

I shoot Harper a look. She leans in and talks lowly, so only I can hear.

"Don't worry, Mason and Vincent are still coming," she assures me.

But I don't feel all that assured, suddenly reminded of the awkwardness that can come of dating, then breaking up with, a coworker. Yeesh.

"Have you thought about how it would be? If you and Mason broke up?" I ask quietly.

Harper leans back in her seat, contemplating that.

"Of course. All I can do is hope that if and

when it happens that we can be adults about it," she replies softly with a shrug.

"Yeah," I murmur. "But to have to run into that person all the time …" I shudder lightly but am saved thinking about it anymore as Mason and Vincent arrive, with Cal just behind them.

Sandwiched between Harper and Sasha, I can only watch as Jules, Ethan, and Mark shuffle out to let Cal sit next to Sasha, squishing me closer to Harper. As I scoot over, I notice Mason is sitting next to her, with Vincent on his other side. I look at Harper, silently wondering why he didn't sit next to me. She gives me an apologetic look back like she knows exactly what I'm thinking and shrugs.

General casual greetings are thrown around the table again. And I don't miss that Vincent barely glances at me. As Mason launches into a story about why they're late, something involving an old guy with Alzheimer's and far more old-man nudity than I wanted to hear about, Sasha leans into me.

"Everything okay with you and Vincent? Why's he sitting over there?"

I roll my eyes and shrug, not making eye contact and trying not to be pissed about it.

"Fine, as far as I know. And I don't know. He's a grown man, he can sit where he wants," I mutter back, taking a deep drink of the cocktail in front of me.

"Then why are you downing that thing like it's liquid patience?" she whispers back pointedly.

This time I look her in the eye, giving her my best irritated glare. She presses her lips together, wisely keeping her trap shut. Cal draws her attention back to him, thankfully, saving her from me.

Because it takes me exactly the time to finish my drink to realize I'm not annoyed. I'm furious. The man has had his head between my damn thighs, and he's sitting over there like we're just coworkers who barely know each other. It wouldn't bother me if he hadn't been the one to come to me, wanting to give this a shot. If I hadn't opened up to him this past week like I can't remember doing with a guy in … I don't know, probably ever.

As soon as Mason is done with his story, though, Mark jumps in.

"That's nothing," he scoffs. "Hey, Becks, you remember when you were prepping that old lady for her screening tests and she ran buck-ass naked through the halls?"

"How the hell could I forget that?" I reply. I bring my hands up to my chest, mimicking the flapping of her huge, sagging breasts as she ran and imitating her raspy soprano. "'If you can't catch me, you can't make me!'"

Everybody bursts out laughing as we continue to recount Mark and I trying to corral her into one of the exam rooms but failing miserably because of the double-entrance setups in all of our rooms.

By the time we're done, everyone is screaming with laughter. Well, not so much Vincent. He's more trying to look anywhere but at me, but I can tell he's chuckling to himself. Mark, who is sitting across from him, is openly wiping tears of laughter from his eyes, and I can't help but be struck by the difference between the two.

Mark has always been interested, and I've never gone there. But he's such a fun, great guy. Why can't I be into someone like that? Someone who isn't afraid to tell people how awesome he thinks I am, like he did the night I officially met Vincent. Someone who will tell stories and laugh with me. Someone who, oh, I don't know, hasn't been to jail and is now pretending like we barely know each other.

My laughter dies when that thought settles in. I withdraw as conversation around the table continues, though every single other person at the table *except* Vincent addresses me directly multiple times. By the end of the night I've got myself pretty worked up.

So when everyone decides to go home, I latch myself onto Jules hoping we can walk each other out so I don't have to deal with it. I don't look at or for Vincent as we leave. I'm just tipsy enough to start a fight but too tired to go there.

She squeezes my arm reassuringly, without me even having to explain. As soon as we're out in the evening air, she leans in.

"I thought you and Vincent were going out now?" she asks quietly and casually.

"Huh," I half laugh, half huff. "Yeah, I thought so too. Not that you would have known it by the way he was acting tonight."

Jules wraps an arm around my shoulders as we find our way into the parking lot. "Maybe he just doesn't want everyone to know yet?" she offers.

I shake my head. "I don't even want to talk about it."

Her hazel eyes look down at me knowingly. "Well, I'm always here. And you're stuck with me a little longer, because I can smell the alcohol on you and I'm driving you home."

I squeeze her around the middle, only because I'm that damn much shorter than her. "Thanks, big sis."

And I know I've had too much to drink when I get in her car and snuggle down into the seat, suddenly mentally, emotionally, and physically done.

I manage to stay awake long enough to get home and climb into bed, though still fully dressed, when my phone pings with a text. A glance tells me it's the last person I want to hear from right now.

Can I come over?

With a snort, I tap out a quick response.

Fuck no.

And, well pleased with myself, I turn off my phone and pass out.

12

———

hankfully, for once, I have Saturday off, so I sleep in and enjoy some much-needed time lying around the house in sweats while watching TV and eating ice cream.

I'm not moping, you're moping.

Okay, maybe I'm moping a little bit.

Vincent wants to pretend like I don't exist in front of people we know? Fine. I'll pretend like he doesn't exist, period. That doesn't mean I have to be happy about it.

And he doesn't make it easy either, with so many texts asking what's going on that I finally just turn off my damn phone. Unfortunately, he's clearly as stubborn as I am, because when someone knocks on my door after dinner, I just know in my gut that it's him.

Because it's what I would do if someone was ignoring me.

I don't even get up from the couch.

"Fuck off, Vincent," I call to the door.

"Not until you tell me why," he demands back.

That gets me on my feet and wrenching the door open.

"Are you fucking kidding me?" I snap at him, hands firmly on my hips.

My icy demeanor slips as I take him in, his tanned, muscled arms crossed over his broad chest, which is barely contained by the Rage Against the Machine T-shirt he's wearing. His dark eyes are filled with fire, and I hate him for looking so goddamn good while I'm angry at him.

"I'm not fucking kidding you," he snaps back.

I cross my arms over my chest, mirroring his aggressive posture. "Well, then, I'd be happy to enlighten you," I reply, letting my voice absolutely drip with sarcasm. "You acted like you barely even knew me, like I hardly existed, in front of all our friends last night. I'm not interested in talking to someone who is *that* ashamed to be going out with me. So I think we're done here."

I make to swing the door closed, but he throws up a hand to stop it. With a solid shove, he pushes into the apartment, closing the door behind him. I'm so surprised by the move, and he looks so menacing as he advances on me with wrath written all over his face, that I take a step back.

"I *acted* that way because *you* were the one who said our relationship was none of their business," he says dangerously quietly. "If you think I'm ashamed of you, you obviously haven't been paying attention." He stops in front of me, hands clenched into fists at his sides.

I open my mouth to shoot back when I realize … I *did* say that.

"Well, you didn't have to not talk to me at all," I insist. "You could've just acted normal. You didn't say a damn word to me or even look at me all fucking night. You think people didn't notice?"

His brows draw together. "That *is* how I act

normally," he points out. "Who the fuck noticed?"

"Um, I …" I stutter, flabbergasted. Because I realize he's right. That is how he used to act around me when we didn't really know each other. How he usually acts with everyone unless they engage him directly. "Jules noticed. But … yeah, that may have been because she knows we're going out." I feel a blush creeping up my neck, realizing I may have overreacted. Again.

"So it's none of their business, but you're telling people?" he asks, shaking his head. "Look. I'm a pretty private person, so I was happy to not make it a big thing. If you want to tell your friends, whatever, but you can't have it both ways. Just don't give me the silent treatment because you changed your mind and didn't fill me in."

I look up at him sheepishly, totally deflated. "That's fair," I admit.

He pulls his head back, a confused look on his face. "Really?" he asks. "I mean, I know it's fair, but you're not going to fight me on it more?"

I scoff a laugh. "Do you want me to?"

He gives me an incredulous look.

"Yeah, didn't think so," I tease. "Yes, I told Sasha and Jules. I know I said it's not our coworkers' business, but it really hurt when I thought you didn't want people to know. That that's why you were ignoring me."

His face softens, and he steps into me. "If I'd known that, I would've handled it differently," he murmurs, looking deeply into my eyes. "I hope you know that."

I bite into my bottom lip, the tension totally gone. Well, the angry tension anyway. The sexual tension? That's always there. And now that I'm not angry anymore …

"Yeah? What would you have done?" I ask in a teasing tone.

A smile pulls at his lips and his hands slide around my backside, pulling me into him. His face drops to my neck, nuzzling into me.

"I would've sat next to you, put my arm around you," his murmurs in my ear send tingles down my spine, "thought about all the things I was going to do to you after I got you alone." His lips slide across my earlobe, and my core tightens as my breath speeds up.

"Show me," I breathe.

He pulls back so he can look into my eyes. "Really?"

Unable to speak under the intensity of his gaze, I nod.

I don't even have time to revel in the anticipation before his mouth is on mine, his tongue insistently pushing past my lips as his hands lift me into his strong arms.

I wrap my legs around his waist, my hands tight around his neck as our tongues slide together in a hard, hot dance that says things are about to start going very not slow anymore.

Between heated kisses that send me spinning, I manage to navigate him to the bedroom. I get a moment to breathe as he drops me on the bed, tearing his shirt off as soon as I've hit the mattress.

And holy. Fucking. Shit. Sculpted, tanned, and tattooed, his torso is the definition of perfection. The thick, muscled arms I've seen plenty of times lead into the most defined set of shoulders I've ever seen. And it never even occurred to me that collarbones could be so erotic. But somehow his are, sharp and dipping into a hollow in the middle of his chest that frames his pecs perfectly. The man is walking sex.

Just like the dark trail of hair that walks to the top of his jeans that he's now rapidly unzipping and pulling down. I watch, mesmerized as his dick springs free, hard and ready, and perfectly sized.

And I can't help myself. I pounce, closing my lips around him and using my hands on his ass to push his shaft deep into my mouth. He gathers my curls in his hands, holding them behind me while he groans into the pleasure.

I slip a hand around to hold the base of his cock while I work so I can look up at him, so I can watch him enjoy this like he's watched me twice before.

His eyes, deep pools of inky darkness, glower down at me so sexily it takes my damn breath away. I keep working him with my hand until he sucks in his own sharp breath, tipping his head back.

I half want to make him come like this, but there will be time for that later. Right now, I need to ride this gorgeous creature until he's screaming my name. Until I get a reaction out of this stoic man. *My man.*

The thought sends a surge through me. A possessive passion I've never felt before.

I rise to my knees, pulling him onto the bed and pushing his chest until he falls backward on the mattress. I finish tugging his jeans and boxers off, then quickly strip off my T-shirt and sweats.

He stares at me, resting a hand behind his head, then playing with one of my nipples with his other hand.

I dip down to lick up his length, then crawl up his body until our mouths meet again. Both of his hands move to cup my face as I settle over him, straddling him.

Thankfully, we've already had *the talk,* so I know he's safe, and lord knows I've been on the pill since I was old enough to sneak off to Planned Parenthood on my own.

So it's with no hesitation that I slip a hand between us, positioning him exactly where I want him. But just to torture him, I rub his tip over me, teasing us both with it.

His head tilts back again, and he sucks in another breath.

"You like that?" I tease, licking my lips in anticipation.

His head tilts back toward me, his eyes flying open.

And with a merciless swing of his hips, he buries himself inside me, causing me to gasp and brace my hands on his chest as he fills me.

"You like that?" he asks back huskily.

I narrow my eyes at him, pushing myself upright. And with a twist of my hips, I pay him back in full. His cock shifts inside me, and we're both rendered speechless again. But as much shit as I talk, there's a time when there is no need for words. And right now, all I need to say I can say with my body.

My hips talk for me, moving over him, back and forth, until I'm soaking wet and writhing with pleasure. His hands find my nipples as I gyrate, pinching and pulling, working me as I work over him. I feel the pleasure start to build, and I hadn't realized how much I missed it. An ache spreads like fire not only through my core but through every part of my body. His warms hands trail over my skin like he knows exactly where I need touching.

One slides over the sensitive skin of my side, slipping down to lightly encourage my hips, while he settles the thumb of his other hand between us so that my clit rubs over it with every thrust. It's a move that, without consciously thinking about it, makes me go faster. So I stroke over his digit in an increasing frenzy until, before I can stop it, my orgasm crashes through and over me, and I tighten around him.

As my hips slow, he holds them in his strong hands, continuing to tilt them himself while he flexes into me, rubbing me deep inside. Not for his own pleasure but to keep mine going.

When the wave recedes, I slump forward as he rises to meet me. Our mouths join lazily while his hands push my now-sweaty curls from my face.

With a gentle motion, he holds and rolls me under him, slipping out of my still-pulsating core. The absence gives me a moment to relax before he has me on my back, rearing up to position himself at my entrance once more.

Still panting, I look up at him, every perfect inch of his glowing skin a complete turn on. But his face. His gorgeous, intense expression, his beautiful mouth pulled into a tight bow in concentration, it just undoes me in a way I can't even explain.

So when he slides back in, I'm already a goner, totally lost to this. To him.

I close my eyes, unable to handle watching him take me. I wanted to make him mine. But I didn't consider how much I wanted to be his.

"Becca," he murmurs.

I open my eyes and look up at him.

When our gazes lock, the corner of his lips pulls up in a smile, his hand reaching to cup my face. When his thumb slides over my lip, I open my mouth to him, take it in, suck it, and clench my legs around him until he's buried completely in me.

His small smile turns into a full grin, and he raises an eyebrow. He removes his now-wet thumb and uses it to work my clit. I gasp and lose my hold of his hips, which he takes as his cue to continue pumping into me.

Like some kind of torture, his strokes seem almost lazy, and his thumb rotates slowly. He watches me carefully until I'm squirming with the need for more.

And then he gives it to me. But only a little at a time. When I feel the beginnings of another orgasm, my breath hitches. Clearly, it's the cue he was waiting for.

He drops down, his mouth meeting mine as our bodies fully merge. His strong arms lock around me, carefully balancing his weight so he can both run his tongue over every part of my upper body and tilt his hips into me at a dizzying pace. Since he's laid over me, every thrust slides him over my clit, setting my orgasm off as if it were a speeding freight train.

Like a ton of bricks, it hits, white-hot pleasure licking through every vein, every inch, every pore of my body. Without thought, I hold onto him for dear life, not sure how I can withstand the level of pleasure coursing through me. A wave of dizziness washes over me as it peaks, and I groan with the strain of keeping myself together. Or at least it feels like that — like if I don't try, I'll come apart at the seams.

Through it all, I can feel him still gaining speed, pounding into my tightened core until his own orgasm takes him. On his final push, I feel the muscles of his back clench as he groans my name into my neck.

His release is my release, and I finally cascade down from my peak, the descent no less pleasurable as I feel his still-hard cock pulsing in my quivering pussy. It adds to the eroticism of our spent, entwined bodies, as we both gasp for breath in the wake of the intensity of the experience.

After my breathing has returned to normal, I'm still lying under him, wrapped in his scent, relishing the feel of his skin when something shifts.

I giggle, pressing a hand to his chest. "As much as I want to stay like this forever, we need to get up or we're going to ruin the bedspread," I tell him.

With a smile and a light kiss on my nose, we pull a quick maneuver to avoid the mess.

When I've cleaned up in the bathroom, I walk back into the bedroom to find him still completely naked, the bedspread thrown back.

"Goddamn, you're fine," I murmur as I approach.

He sits up, readily accepting me into his arms as I slide into the bed next to him.

"And you're a fucking goddess," he tells me, stroking my cheek with his thumb.

"Mmm, you sure know how to make a girl feel special," I hum under his touch.

"Yeah, well, I had to prove I *could*," he teases. "You know, after apparently coming off like a total dickhead."

I look up at him. "Hey, water under the bridge," I assure him. "As long as we can do that again. Soon."

"Demanding little thing, aren't you?" he teases.

I smack his chest indignantly. "Hey, I'm not little," I gripe.

"If you say so," he says with a grin.

I shoot him some stink eye. But I leave it there. I'm too spent to admit it, but I have a theory that my personality is so big to make up for being so short. But I don't like being called little, even if I know I am. In any case, right now, I just want to lie here, touching this gorgeous man and pretending like the roller-coaster that has been our relationship wasn't a thing. And that this bliss, right now, is all that matters. In a way, it is.

"It's not my fault," I reply. "It's my mom's."

"Yeah? She as beautiful as you are?" he asks, rubbing his thumb softly over my arm.

I trace a hand lightly up his abs. "Have you always been such a charmer?"

He giggles and swats my hand away. *Ticklish.* Interesting.

"Just stating facts," he replies.

"Mmm. Yes, well. I do look a lot like her. Except lighter. She's full Puerto Rican, and my dad is Irish-Italian."

"Well, that explains a lot," he says drily.

I smack him hard on the chest and look up to find him smirking down at me.

"Stuff it, guido," I snipe at him.

He laughs unreservedly at my insult. "Guido? I find that funny coming from a girl who's also part Italian," he teases.

I shrug. "I have four batshit-crazy older brothers. If I learned anything growing up, it's how not to take shit from muscleheads."

"Damn, four? Should I be worried?" Though he seems anything but, still tracing a hand lazily over my arm and side.

"Not in the least," I assure him. "I'm sure you guys will get along swimmingly. You'll probably be a hero in their eyes for putting up with their pain-in-the-ass little sister."

I feel his body stiffen a fraction. "You want me to meet your family?"

I shift away and prop myself up on an elbow so I can look at him. "I was just talking," I say, trying to sound as casual as I can. Not wanting to admit that I'm dying to see how he'd manage against the insanity of basically me times six. Lord knows that's the true test of whether he's a keeper.

He lifts a hand up and traces a finger down my cheek. "I didn't mean it like that. I'd love to meet them sometime," he says softly.

And I swear, my heart fucking melts. But I rein it in.

"What about you? What's your family like?" I ask.

He shrugs and pulls himself up so he's leaning against the headboard.

"My mom left when I was seven. My dad's a construction worker. And a total pussy. We never really got along. Can't say I was sad to leave New York," he responds, clearly uncomfortable.

"Really? That's a pretty big change. There wasn't anything else to stay for?" I ask, purposely avoiding the can of worms that he just cracked open. Because as much as I want to know why his mom left, why he doesn't get along with his dad, I also don't want to make him talk about something that clearly bothers him.

"There are always reasons to stay. But I had

to leave," he responds, looking at me intently. "Can't say I'm mad about it right now." He gets a predatory glint in his eye and laces his fingers with mine.

Gently, he tugs me close, his lips softly caressing mine. And as he slides his hard body against me, even though I'm pretty sure he just distracted me out of asking more questions, can't say I'm mad about it either.

13

"**B**oy, when you end a drought, you don't go by half measures," Sasha mutters, continuing to enter patient data despite the deep blush she still has from hearing about the rest of my weekend which was, naturally, spent naked.

I let out a happy sigh. "What can I say? The man is … damn, Sash, I don't even have words."

She chuckles. "There's a first."

"I'm so happy right now, I don't even care that you just insulted me," I reply airily, gathering an armful of files.

"Oh, good. Then you won't mind running the hazmat drop for me after you're done with those," Sasha replies with a big, cheery smile.

I wrinkle my nose at her. It's everyone's least favorite chore around here. Not because the collection itself is difficult. But the guy who runs the disposal unit is a total creep.

"Come on," she coaxes, sensing my hesitation. "You'll have to walk right by intensive care."

"Oh, I'll do it. But only because you're basically in charge right now and you know I can't say no," I reply.

She gives me a knowing look. "Yeah. Okay. Whatever you've got to tell yourself, Becks." She gives me a sly wink and turns back to her monitor.

I huff and roll my eyes, but the files are getting heavy, so I just stomp off to take care of them. Once that's done, I do the rounds, empty all the hazmat bins, and load them up to take them to the disposal unit across the hospital.

As I push the cart through the network of hallways connecting each unit, I shake my head at Sasha's silly appeal to my hormones. The odds of seeing Vincent are practically nil.

And, as expected, I make it to the drop-off having seen only a few other hospital staff along the way.

I tolerate Creepy Kyle's lecherous stare as I unload, thankful that one of the first things Cal did when he started at Rutherford was to get administration to take sexual harassment around here seriously. So even though, when I walk away with my empty cart, I still feel like I need to take a shower, at least I didn't have to throw any punches due to wandering hands.

Oh, yeah, it's happened. The women working in this hospital have long been wary of the dangers of bending over, but sometimes it has to happen.

Thankfully, it's not like he could admit why he got punched without getting himself in trouble. But still. Working in a hospital should be classified as a contact sport. And that's even before anything having to do with patients.

As I'm about to round the corner to the hall between intensive care and cardiac, I hear a feminine laugh. One I know. Avery.

Lo and behold, as soon as I make the turn, I see her, clearly flirting — with *Mason*. My past issues with Harper aside, there's no way in hell I'm going to let this bitch flirt with my friend's man.

"So do you just pretend to prefer women so

you can hit on the guys your friends are with?" I ask in the nastiest tone I can manage as I approach. Avery turns, clearly surprised. "Oh, wait, my bad. Your *former* friends."

I shoot a look at Mason, wondering why he's even talking to this bitch. He doesn't look the least bit guilty, so I guess he's just clueless. Boys.

I stop my cart and fold my arms over my chest, arching an eyebrow.

"We were just talking," Avery scoffs. "Not that it's any of *your* business."

"Bitch, please," I scoff. "Flipping that greasy hair, using that fake, 'Oh, you're *so* interesting,' laugh. Stop embarrassing yourself."

Avery turns red, and Mason glances help-lessly between us.

"I should really get back to work …" Mason shuffles back a couple of steps. "But hey, you and Vincent are meeting us for dinner tonight, right?"

My lips tighten. Vincent had gotten me to agree to it. Since my friends knew, he wanted his best friend to know too. And though I was reluc-tant to bring Harper in on the current state of our relationship, Avery is the absolute last person I'd want to know.

And by the triumphant, catlike grin on her face, she's perfectly aware of the juicy bit of gossip that just landed in her lap.

Motherfucker.

"Yes, we'll see you later," I reply tersely, giving him a pointed glare.

He looks confused but retreats quickly, disappearing down the hall toward emergency.

Avery folds her arms over her chest, mimicking my posture. But looking a whole fuckload smugger.

"So you managed to trick pretty boy into going out with you, huh? Guess we'll see how long *that* lasts," she says meaningfully. And I can just tell the bitch plans to make another play for him.

"Why don't you run along and go find someone who *isn't* taken to fuck?" I suggest archly. "You know, instead of playing with fire."

"Oh, please, I have no intention of fucking Mason," she scoffs. "Vincent, on the other hand — now, he is entirely fuckable."

"Oh, he definitely is," I assure her. "More than you'll ever know."

"We'll see about that," she murmurs, holding my glare. "But right now there are some people I should talk to." The evil glint in her eye as her smile turns nasty tells me she's about to go do exactly what I knew she would the moment the words tumbled out of Mason's mouth.

"You do you, girl. But don't say I didn't warn you," I reply quietly. I park the cart against the wall and breeze past her through the doors to intensive care.

At the very least, I need to warn Vincent that by the end of shift the whole hospital is going to know we're together.

"I'm going to fucking kill Mason." Vincent's jaw ticks against the tightness with which he's clenching it.

"He doesn't deserve to die for being stupid," I reply levelly. "Avery, on the other hand ..." My own jaw feels like it's about to fall off. But all we can do is glower. The small, quiet corner we found to talk has no guarantee of privacy.

"You don't get it," he spits, uncharacteristically venomously. "For you, this is just gossip.

People knowing more than you want them to. For me …" He trails off, shaking his head resolutely.

I frown, unsure why this would get him in so much trouble. "It's not against policy," I assure him, though he must already know that since so many of our coworkers are dating one another. "So it's not like we're going to get fired. Is it really a problem for," I drop my voice to a whisper, "your parole?" I find it hard to believe it would be, but then, what do I know about being on parole?

He gives me a hard stare. "It's …" he shakes his head. "It's complicated. But yes, it's a problem. Not that there's anything we can do about it now." He shoves his hands in his pockets and looks away, still shaking his head at regular intervals like he's having some sort of debate with himself. I get the strong sense that there's something else he's not telling me.

"That's not true. We can end this, now, then it was just rumors. This doesn't need to be … I don't think either of us needs more drama," I say flatly. "So if that's what we need to do, that's what we need to do."

When his eyes find mine again, I can see the hurt.

"Is that what you want?" he asks, his voice thick and low.

"Fuck, no. And I sure as hell don't want to let that bitch win."

He blanches at that. "So you'd keep dating me just to spite her?"

I roll my eyes and throw my hands up. "No, dumbass," I chastise him in a low, angry voice. "I'd keep dating you because I want to date you. Spiting her would just be a bonus."

That gets a quiet chuckle out of him.

"You know, you're pretty fucking cute when you're mad," he murmurs.

"I know," I reply without a hint of modesty, crossing my arms over my chest. "So what do you want, Vincent?"

His dark brows pinch together, his perfect features contorted in worry. "I just want to live my life without worrying about all the bullshit from my past."

I tilt my head at his words, now sure there's more to this story than he's telling me. The sag of his shoulders, the air about him, it all seems … like more than just the parole thing.

"Is your old boss still screwing with you or something?" I ask.

His brows jump in surprise. "Why would you think that?"

I shrug. "I dunno. From his perspective, maybe you got off too light? I just … I feel like there's something else going on here. Something you're not sharing."

I can practically feel his guard go up. Bingo. My intuition never fails me.

He stares at me silently for a minute. I let him. Uncomfortable silence is the bringer of truth, after all.

"I'm sure there are things you haven't shared with me," he finally replies.

"Oh, nuh-uh. You're not going to make this about me," I protest. "There *is* something you're not sharing. And that's fine, but don't play it off like it's no big deal, or like I'm imagining things."

He worries at his bottom lip. "Okay, fine, you're not imagining things," he finally allows. "But now really isn't the time or place."

I fight the urge to take him by the hands. Instead, I pour everything I'm feeling into my expression, hoping he'll understand. "I'm not asking you to spill your guts," I clarify. "I'm just trying to figure out if whatever's going on is going to stop this." I gesture between us. "Because, like it or not, now's the time to figure that out."

He slumps back against the wall behind him. "I can't think as fast as you, Becca. I'm going to need some time."

I look at my watch. "Well, we're supposed to have dinner with your friends in a few hours. So I suggest you get on that."

And I'm such a mixed-up ball of emotions, I don't even have the patience to wait for his response. Instead, I head back to cardiac. Back to ground zero.

As soon as I walk in the doors, I get knowing looks. Damn, that bitch works fast.

I approach the nurses' station to Sasha shaking her head. "This is my fault," she says.

"I see you've already heard," I reply drily.

"Everyone's heard," she responds.

"So how is this your fault?" I ask.

"Well, obviously something happened while you were doing the drop-off. If I hadn't asked you to go —"

I wave a hand, cutting her off. "Let's not

play that game. It is what it is. People were bound to find out eventually."

"Then why do you look so pissed off?" Sasha points out.

With a sigh, I slump into the chair next to her and quietly relay my conversation with Vincent.

"Sweet baby Jesus, Becca, I swear you deal with more drama in a day than I can tolerate in a month," Sasha grumbles.

I shrug. "Most of the time I enjoy it," I admit.

"Except when it's about you," she says perceptively.

"Well, yeah, who wants people messin' in their business?" I reply. "I swear Avery's taken some serious bitch lessons from Lacey."

Sasha's eyes tighten. "Let's hope she's not that bad," she says firmly.

"Hey," I say, catching her eye. She looks at me warily. "Avery can't hurt me, okay? I'm a big girl. I can take whatever she wants to try to throw my way. Don't worry."

Sasha folds her hand over mine. "I know. But I'm a born worrier, Becks. Just ... be careful, okay?"

I put my other hand on top of our hand pile and pat her gently. "I will," I lie.

But Sasha doesn't need to know I'm lying. Or that I plan to find a way to put Avery in her place. Oh, I'll choose my opportunity wisely. But I'll go for it, even if it costs me. Though not if it costs anyone I care about. I may have no regard for the consequences for me, but damned if I'm going to let Avery hurt my people. And right now, it would seem she's already hurting Vincent and trying to hurt Harper. Game. On.

WE END UP GOING TO DINNER WITH HARPER AND Mason, though Vincent still hasn't said a word about the status of our relationship. Needless to say it ends up being pretty tense and awkward. And that's even without me saying anything to Harper about Avery's advances toward Mason. That can wait until the dust settles.

As Vincent silently walks me to my car after, I decide I'm not going to ask for his decision. Not tonight. I don't chase boys. He wants to be with me, he needs to choose that.

I stop at my car door, turning to face him.

"Thanks for walking me out. I'll see you around," I say, trying not to let it sound angry or sarcastic.

He huffs a sarcastic laugh. "You'll see me around? Why does that sound like a 'fuck off'?"

I glare up at him. "What am I supposed to say? You're the one still figuring things out. It's a 'fuck off' if you want it to be one," I say plainly. "But I'm not going to sit around pining after you, hoping you pick me, if that's what you were expecting."

"I wasn't expecting any of this," he shouts, throwing his arms out widely, then running a hand through his hair in agitation. "Fuck, Becca. I'm sorry. I wish I knew what to do right now. What to say."

I shake my head. "If you don't know what to say, that says all I need to know," I reply.

He juts his chin out, his eyes burning into mine. "You don't understand," he responds. "I'm not good at this."

I cock my head to the side. "Good at what, exactly?" I ask.

He steps forward, placing his hands on my arms, looking down at me. "Talking about my feelings," he murmurs. His thumb brushes over my lips. "But I can't lose you."

I close my eyes, my lips pressing against his thumb. "That's all I needed to hear." I open my eyes to find him staring at me.

"Really?" he asks.

"Yes, what did you think I was asking for, a proposal?" I snap. "I just had to know that you're still in this."

"I'm so fucking in this," he breathes, and his mouth drops to mine. His kiss is hungry, desperate, and so overwhelming it makes me dizzy.

I break away to take a breath, to calm my racing heart, but he presses me against the car and grabs my face, bringing it back to his. His intensity is off the charts, and within minutes, we're both so worked up we can barely breathe.

"Take me home," I demand.

He stares down at me. "I was thinking I might just fuck you right here."

My breath catches in my throat. "The last thing we need is for you to get arrested for public indecency," I point out, despite the dampness between my legs agreeing it would very much like him to take me right now.

He buries his face in my neck. "Dammit, you're right," he agrees.

"Then let's go, for fuck's sake," I groan in frustration.

With a chuckle, he pulls back, letting me get in the car.

"I'll follow you," he assures me with a light peck on my lips, then closes the door.

I have to take a few deep breaths as I watch him walk away. I'm practically shaking with desire. And if I get into an accident on the way home, that will delay getting that gorgeous man naked.

So I drive very, very carefully.

14

"He picked you," Harper gushes. "That's so romantic, Becca."

"Let's not make it a big thing," I hedge, rolling my eyes. Even though I secretly agree, and kind of loathe myself for it. "We're just going to give it a shot. Despite the drama."

"Yeah, but you know Rutherford. Someone else will do something and be the new gossip du jour. The attention won't be on you two for very long," she replies.

I pick at the fries on my plate. "I hope not," I admit. "And I have to be honest, I've kind of lost my taste for gossip, so that can't happen soon enough."

Harper puts down the soda she had halfway to her lips, looking beyond stunned.

"You've … lost the will to gossip?" she asks in a dramatic whisper, a hand fluttering to her chest. "Are you feeling okay? Should we get you back to the hospital?"

"Ha. Ha. Ha," I snip. "Look, that's not why I asked you to dinner tonight. I need to tell you what else happened with Avery on Monday."

Harper picks her soda back up. "It's okay, Mason told me."

I shoot her a skeptical look. "Oh, yeah? What, exactly, did he tell you?"

"That she was hitting on him. Which apparently he didn't get until you came along." She rolls her eyes. "Boys."

I let out a laugh. "Well, I'm glad he told you, anyway. I don't know what I'm going to do about her, but she's gotta be stopped."

Harper shrugs. "I'm honestly not that worried about it. The more attention you give her, the more power she has over you."

"That's surprisingly mature of you. Aren't you worried she's going to keep coming after your man?" I ask.

She laughs. "Becca, he didn't even get that

that's what she was doing. I'm *so* not worried about it," she replies. "Are you, really? Because I've seen how Vincent is around you. He's totally smitten. I don't think you have anything to worry about. I mean, she took a shot before, right? And he didn't bite."

A memory from last night of Vincent's teeth on my neck surfaces, and I smile. But Harper can be even more of a prude than Sasha, and the good lord knows we're not as close, so I don't say anything.

"You're right," I agree. "I guess I just have a hard time letting that shit go."

"I'm a big believer in karma," Harper says. "And Avery's got lots of it coming her way, don't you worry. And if we're really lucky, we'll get to watch." She grins, and it's almost evil. But I know she's a little too well-meaning to really want to hurt someone. Though intentions aside, we're all capable of hurting people.

"Well, I don't trust her, but I guess I don't have to be the one to dish out her just desserts," I finally agree. "But damn, it's going to be hard to just not do anything. Girl's gone after both our men *and* participated in that whole Lacey-Sasha madness."

Harper's features pinch together. "Yes, but so did I," she reminds me with sadness in her voice.

I point a finger at her. "You did, but you regret it. You've apologized, and now you're showing us that we can trust you again," I correct her.

She beams at me. "Yeah?" she asks hopefully.

"Yeah," I reply with a wink. A comfortable silence falls for a minute, while we regard each other. And the thought that we're finally getting back to where we were improves my mood considerably. "Now. The next important question: What should we have for dessert?" I pluck the dessert menu from the caddy at the back of the booth and lay it out between us.

"Oh, that's easy: The answer to all important questions is chocolate," she teases, pointing at the chocolate fudge brownie pie a la mode, the only chocolate option on the page.

"Well, I certainly can't argue with that," I reply with a laugh.

We order our dessert and spend the rest of the evening on less stressful topics. By the end of the night, I'm thinking Harper is right. Life's short, and I've got the guy. I need to let it go. Avery can fuck off for all I care. Though I do still hope that when karma comes for her, I do actually get to see it.

THE REST OF THE WEEK GOES BY IN THE USUAL bustle of patients, admin duties, and, unfortunately, still dealing with gossip and looks, as nothing juicier has come up.

But Friday happy hour is the complete opposite of last week. Vincent makes sure to sit next to me, holding my hand and otherwise making it obvious that we're a couple. If I'm being honest with myself, it makes me nervous. Especially when I see how happy Sasha is watching us acting all couple-y. She even makes me promise that we'll go on a double date soon. Yeesh.

But going home with Vincent afterward wipes it all from my mind, as usual. I may have reservations about the whole being-in-a-real-relationship thing, but we have no issues on the sex front. In fact, it's where things flow the best. Where we just fit. But still in a much deeper, more meaningful way than I'm used to. Though when we're together, absorbed in each other, I find it much easier to let it be what it is and not think too hard about it. In short, it's still my favorite thing, even in the context of a relationship. I guess I shouldn't be that surprised.

We even double date with Harper and Mason again on Saturday night, which I *don't* tell Sasha as I'd hemmed and hawed about doing that with her and Cal. But that's different — Sasha is practically like family to me. And I'm not quite ready to go there with Vincent. Not until we get to know each other better.

Sunday is half spent having sex, half getting to know more about each other, though in a pretty casual way. Like, what were our favorite TV shows growing up. Which bones we've broken. Places we've worked. That kind of crap. All good stuff, but still light enough not to be too scary, too deep, too … commitment-y. If that's a word.

Still, I can't remember the last time I dated the same guy for two weeks. It's definitely been a minute. Which, I know, is all kinds of messed up in and of itself. In any case, this guy has been different from the start. Because I've been into him for more than three months, so he was already a record for me. Well, not counting Jimmy Dugan in fifth grade. I was into that dude the whole school year until he saw my bra strap at our elementary school graduation and made fun of me. As if wearing a training bra wasn't already awkward enough. He's also the first boy I had an actual fistfight with, because even then I didn't take shit from anybody. Though I think the odds of that happening with Vincent are pretty low.

Thankfully, on Monday morning, one of the PAs from maternity becomes the instant star of the gossip circuit when it gets out that he was arrested for hiring a prostitute. Whom he had sex with *at the hospital*. Hospital workers have hard jobs, so we love nothing more than some good, stress-relieving gossip. But it's so much more exciting when something happens on premises. Maybe because it's so much more real? I don't know. Either way, it's a hot topic, and Vincent and I finally get relief from scrutiny.

I'm practically giddy waiting for him to come over after work, having felt a lightness all day at being out of the spotlight.

So when I answer the door to find him showered and changed into his usual jeans and tee, I practically jump him.

"Well, I'm glad you waited until we were alone," he jokes as he enters the apartment. "I think we've all learned a little lesson about getting busy at work today." The grin on his face is infectious, so I give him a teasing pinch as I smile back.

"Someone's feeling peppy," I tease him.

He shrugs, trying to appear nonchalant and totally failing. "I can't say I love working at the hospital, but I have a new appreciation for working there and *not* being the juicy gossip of the moment."

I tug him into the living room, crashing onto the couch. "God, you're telling me. I got so much done today. Plus, there was the sunshine and birds chirping and all of that again," I joke.

He settles in next to me, slinging an arm around my shoulder.

"So, do they ever go back to old gossip?" he asks curiously.

I shake my head. "Nah, there will always be something new and more exciting for them to latch onto now," I assure him. "I think things are back to normal for good."

"Good," he says with a sigh of relief. "I like normal."

"Hey, before I forget," I say. "Sasha asked if we wanted to get dinner with her and Cal on Wednesday. You know, so they can get to know you."

I look up at him, trying to hide how nervous even asking that question makes me. And when he shifts uncomfortably, I can't help the knots in my stomach that suddenly squeeze tightly.

"I, uh …" he mumbles. "I can't do Wednesday. I … I check in with my parole officer on Wednesdays."

I raise an eyebrow at the tension that has seized him. "Okay," I reply. "You don't have to be embarrassed about that."

"I know. It's just … not something I really want them to know," he responds.

"Don't worry, I'm not going to tell them anything you don't want me to," I assure him. "Sasha may be one of my best friends, but you're important to me too. And I mean, if you don't want to go out with them at all, that's … I mean, that's okay."

I kind of choke on the words, because it's really not okay. At least, not if we really have hope of this working. Because I can't even imagine Sasha not liking someone I'm with. It's part of why I'm so nervous about them getting to know each other. Probably even more so than him meeting my actual family, whom I only see every once in a while when my mom nags me to visit.

"Hey," he says, folding his hand over mine. "It's not that. Just … another time, okay?"

I look up into his eyes and nod.

"Okay," I reply softly.

"I'm sorry, I didn't mean to bring down the mood," he apologizes, pushing a stray curl behind my ear.

"You were just being honest," I reply with a shrug. "It's all good."

"Hmmm," he hums. "I think I know how to make it better."

I raise an eyebrow. "Yeah? How's that?"

A wicked grin spreads across his gorgeous face as he topples me back onto the couch.

"Just you lie back, relax, and I'll show you," he promises, kissing me lightly on the lips before moving his mouth down my body.

I dimly register that he's distracting me with sex. Right before I remember that I don't give a damn why, as long as he keeps his amazing hands on me and uses that talented tongue of his. Which is exactly what he proceeds to do, and everything else melts away.

My week continues to be epic until Thursday afternoon, when I walk into the break room for more coffee only to find Avery there.

"Oh, Becca, I'm so glad we ran into each other," she says in a sweet voice that somehow has a sharp edge to it.

Not one to be deterred from a necessary caffeine fix, I ignore her in favor of the coffee machine.

"Well, I thought you might be a little reluctant to talk to me, so I guess I'll be the one doing the talking," she finally says. "You'll never guess where I saw your boyfriend last night."

As the coffee drips into my cup, I roll my eyes. Great. She saw him go into the courthouse to meet his probation officer. Thankfully, unless she saw him *inside* the courthouse, it's unlikely that she knows why he was actually there.

"Oh, I know where he was last night," I

assure her without turning around. "But thanks for your concern."

"Wow. I wouldn't be okay with my partner visiting a prostitute, but damn, if that's how you guys do things, I guess that's all you," she says sarcastically.

It's a good thing I'm not holding a cup of hot liquid yet, because that causes me to spin around.

"Why the fuck would you think he was visiting a prostitute at the courthouse?" I hiss, trying not to yell. And hoping like hell she's not spreading that whopper around.

"The courthouse? Who said anything about a courthouse?" she asks. "No, no. I saw him go into the house of a known prostitute in National City yesterday."

"You're such a liar, Avery," I spit at her. "Even if he was in National City for some reason, how in the hell would you even know this person was a prostitute?" Though my mind is already scrambling for an explanation. Maybe that's where his parole officer lives? Though I toss that out quickly. Surely he'd have to check in at an official location. And why would a parole officer be a suspected prostitute?

"I'm staying there with my aunt," she responds before my brain can make any sense of this. "A car parked in front of her house yesterday around five. Your boyfriend got out and went down the road, into a house on the other side of the street. The woman who lives there has been a prostitute for years. Everyone in the neighborhood knows it. He clearly parked far enough away so his car wouldn't be associated with that house, and he was in there for a couple of hours too. She must be something if he —"

Before I know it's even happening, my hand cracks sharply across Avery's face. I should be horrified that I slapped her. I should be worried about getting fired. But right now, I'm red-hot raging mad.

"How *dare* you," I seethe, seeing right through her. "You can't have him, and you don't want me to either, so you make up this bullshit? You're just as bad as Lacey. You're going to ruin his life if you go around telling people these lies, Avery."

She steps closer, her cheek flaming red and swollen.

"He told you he was going to the courthouse,

did he?" she whispers, putting it together. "Well, maybe next time he's supposed to be 'at the courthouse,' you should follow him. Then you'll see that I'm *not lying*."

I laugh in her face. "You're delusional. Even if he is going to someone's house, I'm supposed to, what, go up to her once he's gone and accuse her of being a prostitute? Yeah, that'll go real well. I don't know what game you're trying to play, but it's not going to work."

Avery stares at me. "Look. We were friends once, Becca, so I'm going to try to forget all the shit that's been going down between us lately for just a minute. You barely know this guy. And I'm telling you the truth. If it were me, I'd want to know. So I'll tell you what. I won't breathe a word of this to anyone. Then you have all the space you need to figure out that I'm being honest. And that, while it did make me happy to think it might ruin your fun because you've been such a bitch to me lately, I'm *not* Lacey."

"*I've* been a bitch? You went after Vincent when you knew I liked him," I snap.

"But it made you do something about it, didn't it?" she insists.

I can't help the laugh that escapes me.

"Don't even try to pretend that's why you did it. If you want to avoid the Lacey comparisons, maybe try not sounding like such a lunatic," I reply. "And about that. Did Lacey finally fuck you over too? Because last I checked you were her happy little lap dog."

Avery's nostrils flare and her eyes narrow. "I did my best to give her the benefit of the doubt. She was my friend. I don't just turn my back on friends without my own proof," she responds, her voice laced with accusation.

"Are you saying that's what I did? Because that's fucking rich," I retort. "Unlike you, I don't need solid proof that someone is no good. Actions speak pretty clearly for themselves."

Her sinister smile returns. "Oh, you mean, like visiting a hooker? Yeah, that speaks loud and clear," she replies matter-of-factly. "My break is up, and your coffee is getting cold. Good luck with your boyfriend. You're going to need it."

With that, she turns and leaves.

When I return to the nurses' station, still furious and with a lukewarm cup of coffee, I find a slip of paper on my chair. On it is an address in National City. I crumple it in my fist furiously, but before I can make my way to the garbage can, Dr. MacDougall comes around the corner. So instead, I shove it in my pocket and slide into my seat, pretending like I'd been working all along. He stops to have a conversation with Dr. Franklin, and by the time they're done I've managed to actually get back to working. It takes all of my focus to keep going to the end of the day without punching someone or something, but somehow I manage.

15

Avoiding Vincent on Thursday evening is easy enough. It's not like we hang out every night.

While I don't necessarily believe Avery, it's a hard thing to just shake off. And a hard subject to broach with a guy you've been dating for only a few weeks. Especially when there are things you still don't know about him. Things he doesn't want to share yet. Things you hope have nothing to do with prostitutes.

As I sit at the nurses' station desk on Friday afternoon, with happy hour looming, I know I'm not going to be able to pretend like Avery didn't just drop the hooker bomb.

"Hey," a soft voice says, cutting into my thoughts. I look up to find Jules, with her arms resting serenely on the countertop, her auburn hair pulled back into a sleek ponytail, her hazel eyes examining me with concern. "You okay?"

I give her my best attempt at a smile. "Nothing a little booze won't fix," I reply flippantly.

She tilts her head, clearly seeing right through my bullshit. As usual.

"Then let's go," she replies, pulling the band out of her ponytail and letting her long hair go free.

"We've still got a half hour," I gripe. "And how do you look like a fucking hair model at the end of the day," I point up at my crazy bun, "while I look like I have an octopus trying to escape out of the top of my head?"

Jules laughs as she rubs her scalp. "If it helps, I *feel* like I have an octopus trying to escape out of the top of my head," she assures me. "And you know I have the power to dismiss you early. So, what do you say? We'll go ahead of the crowd. I'll buy you a drink. And you can tell me what's on your mind. We haven't gotten to talk just you and me in a while, Becca. Please?"

With a sigh, I look back at the computer screen, realizing I wasn't about to get anything done anyway, so I shut it off.

"Don't have to ask me twice," I say with a forced smile, rising to grab my purse. "But when I take my hair down, no laughing when it doesn't go like a Pantene commercial."

Jules presses her lips together and makes a crossing motion with her fingers over her heart. "Deal."

With a smirk, I let my bun loose, sending curls poofing everywhere. As crazy as it must look, it feels damn good. And it's one of my favorite things about the end of a workday.

"You want to change?" she asks as we head down the hall, knowing scrubs aren't my preferred look outside of the hospital.

I shake my head. "Just get me to the liquor," I joke.

She shoots me a worried glance that I choose to ignore. I'm not opening this can of worms within earshot of anyone we work with.

"That's … that's …" Jules sputters.

I polish off the martini in front of me, waiting for her to finish her sentence. She doesn't, but I get what she means. It's a lot.

"Yep," I agree.

"Do you believe her?" she asks.

"Do I believe Avery that my … whatever the hell he is went to see a prostitute?" I shake my head, looking grimly down into my empty glass. "I don't want to. But how do I just ignore that kind of information?"

Jules lays a hand over one of mine, and I look up.

"I hate to put this so bluntly, but you either trust him or you don't," she points out.

"Then I guess I don't," I reply with a shrug.

"Okay, weird question," Jules hedges. I gesture for her to continue. "Is it him you don't trust? Or men?"

I let out a sharp laugh. "Well, don't you just get right to it?" I smile, spinning the empty glass in my hands while I consider that. "Men."

"You want to trust him."

I look up through tears. "Yes," I admit. "I do. But I grew up with a mother and father who only kept their hands off each other long enough to fight, not giving a shit if their kids heard or saw any or all of it, and four brothers who talked loudly and proudly about each of the many 'sluts' they banged. Respect and trust weren't exactly the norm at the Dillon house, especially coming from the men."

"So you think all men are like your father and brothers?" she presses.

I huff a laugh. "Not at first. But the more I dated, the more it seemed that way. Until him."

Jules smiles sadly. "It's always 'until,' my dear. Until you value yourself. Until you find someone who values you. Until you stop letting your past dictate your future," she says.

"Speaking from experience, are we?" I ask sarcastically. Then immediately regret it. "I'm sorry, Jules, I didn't mean it."

She leans back in her chair, crossing her long, slim legs. "No, that's fair," she allows. "I don't have the best track record with men, and at some point I just stopped trying. But I've seen how you've changed since you've been into this guy. I thought it was a good thing, but some of the things you've told me tonight make me wonder. Though that doesn't mean it still can't be."

"Why'd you think it was a good thing?" I ask curiously.

"Well, the rotating door of hookups stopped," she responds drily. "I always figured that'd be the sign you found The One."

That gets a chuckle out of me. "Honestly, I was over it before him."

"So you were already ready for the next thing. But I know you — you don't settle for just anyone. Which means there's something between you and this guy," she says. "Do you think it's worth trying to make it work?"

"I want it to. But I don't even know how to have those kinds of conversations with a dude," I admit. "I'm terrified, Jules. That I'm going to scare him off. Or worse, that it's true." I slump my head onto the table, then abruptly spring back up at the stickiness. "Okay, that was a bad idea." I grab a napkin, rubbing furiously at my forehead while Jules laughs.

"Well, news flash, kiddo," she replies. "Nobody really knows how to have those kinds of conversations. They're always hard, and they're always awkward as hell. If you care enough about being in a relationship with him, and he with you, you guys will get through it. If not, it wasn't meant to be."

"Ya think?" I ask hopefully, starting to realize for the first time that I do want to talk to Vincent about it. I've just never been in a position like this. Never wanted to talk through things. Never had anything to talk through.

"I don't think, I know," she replies firmly. "But I do have one question."

I raise an eyebrow. "Okay …"

"Is there a reason you haven't told Sasha any of this?" she asks softly.

I scrunch my face up. "Honestly? Because I don't think she'd really understand," I admit. "I mean, I know she's got my back. But this is new territory for me, and I just felt like … I don't know, it might make it worse?"

"Yeah, she is kind of in her little Cal bubble," Jules says. "I'm happy for her, but I know what you mean. Although … maybe you should go talk to your mom."

I blanch at the suggestion.

"Where the hell did that come from?" I ask

sharply. Jules knows about the love-hate relationship I have with my family, and my mother in particular. I love her, don't get me wrong, but my dad isn't the only one she fights with constantly. She and I have gone at it something fierce many times over the years. At some point I decided it just wasn't worth dealing with it to try to have a close relationship with her.

"Hear me out," she pleads. "You have this perception of your family that's affected your relationships with men. But have you ever talked to her about it as an adult?"

I shake my head. "You know that woman and I are like match and kindling."

"Maybe. But she might have insights that surprise you. She is your mother, after all. And I can't help feeling like she may have more of a role in your mistrust of men than you think." Jules purses her lips after she says that, like she's worried she just crossed a line.

I narrow my eyes, not sure I like where she's going. "What, exactly, do you mean by that?" I ask tersely.

Jules takes a deep breath, and I know she's about to go there. "I mean, maybe you're also afraid that you're like your mother. That you're going to end up picking someone like your father," she says. "From the sound of it, you and Vincent have gone through quite a bit of drama already. Maybe you're just as afraid of it working out."

My stomach clenches, and I feel a scowl pull at my face. But I don't know if it's because I agree or disagree.

Scratch that.

"Fuck, I hadn't even considered that," I admit. "And because it pisses me off … you might not be wrong."

Jules shoots me an apologetic look. "I know," she says, and we both laugh a little. "But I know you pretty well, babe. And I've never seen you be afraid of anything for very long. You've got this."

I swallow hard and nod. She's right. I'm a grab-life-by-the-balls kind of girl. I've got this.

"Thanks, Jules," I reply with a sigh.

"More booze?" she asks with a small smile.

"More booze," I agree.

We both get refills and Jules spends the rest of the time until our coworkers show up catching me up on hospital politics and a few bits of gossip I'd somehow missed. All hail the original Gossip Queen. But then, really, I'm backing off that whole scene, and Jules has always had her ear to the ground, what with being so involved and having worked in most parts of the hospital. If I'd ever had an older sister, I imagine she'd have been a lot like Jules. If nothing else, I'm grateful in this moment that I have good friends.

The boost I got from our conversation was necessary to act normally once Harper, Mason, and Vincent show up together, joining me, Jules, Sasha, Cal, Zoe, and Ethan.

Thankfully, once Vincent slides into the booth next to me, it's not like there's time or space for private conversation. But the small touches he uses to keep anchored to me are more comforting than I thought they'd be. Like reassurance that he's real, that's he's with me. And I know that's just as big for him as it is for me.

At some point, Ethan actually manages to engage Vincent in real conversation across the table, and it gives me an excuse to watch him. Well, stare at him, if I'm being honest.

His dark hair is messy from a long workday. His leather jacket drapes over the booth behind him, allowing the white V-neck tee he's wearing to show off the tattoos winding up his chest and down his upper arms. He seems relaxed and at ease, even though conversation isn't usually his thing. And always heartbreakingly gorgeous. And mine. I hope.

He finishes a sentence and catches me staring out of the corner of his eye. His lips tug up into a small smile, and his eyes meet mine. Usually, when he looks at me like that, I can see the desire in his eyes. But this time they're warm and relaxed. The normalcy of it all is like a punch in the gut, because I know I'm going to have to blow apart this sweet spot we've managed to find. But not tonight.

Tonight, I let him take me home.

As soon as we're inside, his fingers lace into mine, pulling me gently into his embrace.

"You were quiet tonight," he murmurs, looking seriously down into my eyes.

"Guess we switched roles," I tease.

He smiles so wide it crinkles the corners of his eyes. "I wouldn't go that far."

"Are you making fun of how much I usually talk?" I reply sassily.

"I wouldn't say 'making fun,'" he hedges with a mischievous smile.

I give him a look back, daring him to say more, but he just laughs. Smart man.

"It was a long week. Guess I'm just tired," I finally reply. It's true, though it's not the reason why I was so quiet.

Vincent advances with me in his arms, causing me to walk backward down the hall to my bedroom.

"I've got just the thing for that," he replies, pushing me through the bedroom door and onto the bed.

"Mmmm, now we're talking," I reply, licking my lips and looking up at him.

"Strip," he demands, tossing his jacket on the chair in the corner and kicking his shoes off.

When that's all he does, I shoot him a disappointed look. "You first."

He walks to the edge of the bed, staring down at me impassively.

"Guess I'm going to have to do it for you, then."

He leans down and removes the scrubs top, then the camisole I'm wearing under it. My scrubs bottoms go next, leaving me in just a bra and panties. But the infuriating bastard is still wearing far too much clothing.

"Lay on your stomach," he directs.

I raise an eyebrow at him while I scoot back and flip over, silently just glad that he didn't push further on why I'm not so much with the talking. I'm happy to fill the silence with sex and have him be none the wiser until I know how I want to handle this. And I try like hell not to think about whether or not he's actually been fucking a hooker while I wait, facedown and mostly naked.

The bed creaks as his weight is added, and I feel him crawling over me until he's settled over my backside, his knees on either side of me. I'm about to look back and ask him what in the holy hell he's doing when his hands land on my shoulders, gently kneading the sore muscles in circles.

"Ohhhh," I groan. "That feels *so* good." I tuck my face back into my arms, giving him better access to my neck.

Strong thumbs slide firmly over the nape of my neck, swirling down my spine. His hands work symmetrically, undoing the knots along my shoulder blades, skimming firmly down my arms then sides, undoing the tension in my lower back. After a good fifteen minutes, he finally slides further back, his hands continuing down my hips, then over my backside.

"Damn, you've got the most gorgeous ass," he murmurs.

I turn my head to look back at him with a smile, feeling much more relaxed. "Glad you're a fan of the big booty," I joke.

"You have no idea," he says, planting his hands firmly on the backs of my knees. In one, swift movement, he pushes them toward the head of the bed, raising my ass in the air.

I squeal in surprise. Before I can protest, he pulls my panties down and spreads my legs open, so I'm exposed to him. His fingers slip between my thighs, and when they dip in my folds, he shakes his head and curses. Like he's surprised that a gorgeous man rubbing me would make me wet. I let out a sigh of pleasure and sink into the mattress.

I'm not surprised this time when his hot, wet mouth meets my skin. He kisses a trail up my thigh, his tongue reaching for my clit. I grind unapologetically into his face, eager for it. He firmly licks in circles until I'm shaking, then pulls away.

I look back, planning on asking for more,

only to see him shirtless, removing his pants. When his gorgeous cock springs free, I have no more words. His eye catches mine as he fists himself, stroking up his length. I nod, silently asking for it, and he climbs behind me, wasting no time as he sinks into me.

We both groan at the perfect, delicious fit. But damn, I need more. I buck my hips, encouraging him to start moving. And he does, sparing nothing as he takes me roughly. The harder he goes, the more helpless I become as my orgasm swirls and churns inside me. I'm practically one with the mattress when I finally come, moaning loudly into the comforter.

He waits until I've relaxed to pull out, rolling me onto my back. Because I sure as hell can't do it myself. I'm exhausted. Emotionally, and now physically, from how hard I've just come. But the sight of him over me, pulling my panties off completely, still hard and ready to take me again gives me a second wind. I open my legs in a silent plea.

Like a magnet, he's back between my legs as if he belongs there, like it took effort for him to *not* be there. And when he slides back in, it feels so fucking good, so fucking right.

Like we were made to do this, just with each other.

As he works over me, the things I'm feeling as he fucks me … it's beyond intense, on every level. And I don't want to name it. Not now. Not while it all feels so …

"Oh, damn," I cry as he leans fully into me, his skin meeting mine, his cock pushing deeper than ever.

"God, yes," he groans in my ear.

We work together, and in moments we're both coming, loudly, insanely, in crazy bursts of white-hot fire burning through our skin. Everywhere he's touching me is on fire with pleasure, until I crash back to earth with him still on top of me.

He strokes my hair away from my face, kissing me gently. His tenderness undoes me, and I feel like I want to cry because I realize on a visceral level that I don't want Avery's claims to be true. I want him to be the man I hope he is. The man who I …

I avoid looking in his eyes, knowing the emotion will just completely shatter me. Because no matter how much I've tried not to think it, especially now, he fucking owns me.

Body, mind, and heart. I don't know when it happened or how. And I know it's probably just about the worst place to be in this exact moment. But it doesn't matter now.

Because I know without a doubt that I'm in love with Vincent DeMarco.

16

The reality of my feelings for Vincent hits me like a ton of bricks, and I realize Jules is right. So much about my past is messing me up right now. And before I can unpack Avery's accusation and what it means for our relationship, I need to get my own head straight.

So here I am, standing on the porch of the house I grew up in. About to open Pandora's fucking box. Vincent wanted to come with me, to meet my family, but I deflected. I need to be here alone if I'm going to get the answers I'm looking for, not bringing him in deeper into my life.

I must have been standing here lost in

thought longer than I realized, because I haven't even knocked when the door swings open. Isabel Feliciano Rodríguez Dillon stares back at me, leaning against the doorframe. It's like looking thirty years into my future: Her dark curls have but a few streaks of grey. Her skin is still smooth. She's a bit rounder in the midsection than when I was a little girl, but her face, her posture, have every bit as much attitude as ever. There was never any question in my mind where I got it.

"I didn't believe you'd actually show up," my mother says in her still-noticeable Puerto Rican accent. Considering she's been here nearly forty years, that's saying something.

"What, a girl can't just come home to visit her family?" I snark back, pushing past her into the house.

I can practically feel her eyes roll behind me as she slams the door shut.

"On a Saturday evening?" she calls after me as I make my way into the living room. "Let's just say it raises some questions."

"Dad home?" I ask, dodging her attempt at getting me to spill the beans right away.

"He and Chris are finishing taking down a

tree in the backyard," she says as I settle onto the old gray couch.

"Didn't this couch used to be blue?" I ask. "Wait … Chris? He's back from New York? When did that happen?" The youngest of my older brothers at just over four years older than me, Chris is a photojournalist who, last I knew, was living in New York City.

"That was a different couch, and yes," she replies, settling down near me. "He's staying with us until he finds a place."

My eyebrows pop up. "So he's *back* back?"

"So it would seem," she replies, crossing her short legs under her. "And I guess I'm glad to hear we aren't the only ones you don't keep in touch with."

"Hey, I call at least once a month," I protest.

My mother shoots me a sharp look. "And say next to nothing," she replies. She shakes her head. "So are you going to tell me what's going on? You're not pregnant, are you?"

I snort a laugh. "No, Mom, I'm not pregnant," I reply impatiently.

She gives me an expectant look, and I sigh.

"Look, I know I haven't come around a lot

lately. And I'm sorry. I've just been busy with work and —"

"Boys?" she guesses.

I fight the urge to snap at her.

"Yes, fine, boys," I admit.

"Mhm. Tell me about him," she replies with a knowing smile.

"What makes you think there's a particular 'him'?" I ask, my walls still firmly up. As much as I came here to talk about exactly this, there's no undoing a lifelong pattern. And I'm not in the habit of having deep talks with my mother. This is going to be difficult, at best.

My mother opens her mouth, no doubt to give a snarky response, but she's cut off by Dad and Chris entering through the back door.

"Izzy?" Dad calls.

My mother levels a look at me before rising to meet my dad in the kitchen. I follow her through the open doorway between the two spaces to find Dad and Chris rummaging through the fridge and cupboards.

"Sean, what are you doing? Get your grubby paws out of there," Mom snaps at him.

Dad straightens up with a grin, and I get a good look at what she's talking about. They're both covered in dirt from head to toe. Chris gives me a little wave behind Dad's back.

"We were thirsty," my dad says defensively.

Chris cocks his head toward the attached dining room, and I follow him while Mom and Dad continue to argue.

"Home, sweet home," I mutter as I sink into a chair at the table across from Chris. He kicks his sweaty, socked feet up on the chair next to him. "Better not let Mom see you do that."

He gives me a cocky smirk. "Nice to see you too, Sis."

I stick my tongue out at him, and it's like we're kids all over again. We both laugh.

"So what happened to New York?" I ask.

He runs a hand tiredly through his dark wavy hair. Like all of my brothers, he looks just like Dad — thick, beautiful hair wholly unlike the wiry and crazy locks Mom and I have, light amber-brown eyes, and skin fair enough to pass for purely European. On top of being pretty easy on the eyes, they all have Dad's charm too. Well, when they want to; otherwise they're usually just assholes. But then, I'm their annoying little sister, so I get more than my share of that sort of thing.

"It was going great until I slept with my boss," he admits.

My brows pull together. "Guy or girl?" I ask. Last I'd heard, he worked for a guy who was starting his own travel magazine, and I didn't think he swung that way. Not that I'd care if he did.

"*She* was a woman," he corrects me with a hard glare. "One of the editors at the Times."

I hold my hands up. "Hey, whatever, it's all good. How come you didn't tell me you were back?"

Mom bursts angrily into the dining area, slamming a glass of lemonade in front of each of us before storming back into the kitchen.

Chris's eyes follow her out as he chugs the drink. "I only got in a couple days ago. And, you know, dealing with Mom and Dad has taken all of my energy."

I snort. "Seriously. It's no wonder I have no clue what a healthy relationship looks like."

Chris's eyes land on mine. "Boy trouble?" he asks slyly.

"Why do you all presume that the only reason I'm here is because of a boy?" I ask angrily.

"Ooh, hit a nerve," Chris says, his grin widening. I forget how much my brothers are like sharks. A little blood in the water and it turns into a feeding frenzy. "Come on, Beck, seriously. You okay? Mom says you don't come around anymore, yet here you are. Something must be up."

I heave a sigh and drop my head on the table dramatically. "Fine, yes, it's a boy."

"So? Do I need to go kick someone's ass? Or is it something else? Need advice?" he asks.

I lift my head and give him a surprised look. "You'd kick someone's ass for me?"

"If that's what you wanted. I've got to make up for being a shitty brother all these years somehow," he replies. He points at my untouched lemonade. "You gonna drink that?"

I roll my eyes and slide it across the table to him.

"You're not a shitty brother," I allow. "Though you weren't the best relationship role model either. Not that that's your fault."

He stops halfway through my drink. "How was I not the best relationship role model? You were like, what, twelve when I moved out?"

"I was fourteen," I correct him. "To be fair, it

wasn't just you. Josh and Justin were bad too. Though none of you hold a candle to Ryan."

Chris rolls his eyes and snorts. "You were a kid. I'm surprised you even remember any of that."

I try not to look hurt. "I was old enough," I reply. "And you guys … well, you weren't exactly shy about graphically describing your exploits with all the skanks you dated."

He gives me the most confused look I've ever seen on his face. "I honestly don't remember it that way at all," he says slowly. "I didn't even kiss a girl until I was eighteen, Beck. Not that that's really any of your business."

My jaw drops. "Then … wait … no," I stutter. "Seriously, Chris, I distinctly remember this. There was this one time, you were talking about Sarah, the girl you took to junior prom, and how she —"

He holds up a hand. "Gave me a blow job in the limo? Yeah, that didn't happen." His ears turn red and he looks behind me, presumably to make sure Mom and Dad aren't within earshot.

"Look, you were young. And yes, there were things said that probably sounded pretty bad. But we were teenage boys, Beck. We talked a lot of shit. And I'm sure we said some not nice things. Do you know why?"

I shake my head, totally bewildered. Chris rubs his dirty hands over his face, then finishes off the lemonade before continuing.

"It may surprise you to know that Ryan was the only one who really got any action when we were growing up. The rest of us … well, I guess we were just trying to live up to him. And Dad. They were both so vocal about … enjoying women. I think we thought we had to be the same way. It was all just talk, though. Stupid, immature, and almost entirely fabricated to impress other people."

"But the way you talked about those women —"

"Was totally and utterly disrespectful," he agrees. "I know. I guess I didn't know that you were paying attention to all that macho bullshit. You might be right — if that's what you heard and took as bible, you really *don't* have any idea of what a healthy relationship looks like."

"That almost sounds like you're agreeing that Mom and Dad aren't exactly role models in that area either," I point out.

He laughs. "I think that's obvious. They've

always been nuts. But, you know, we're adults now. Our relationships are our problems. Just because our parents aren't exactly the paragon of a functional marriage doesn't mean we can't figure out our own shit."

"Doesn't it, though?" I push. "Because I'm finding it kind of difficult to know how to do this whole relationship thing."

Chris's eyebrows shoot to his hairline. "Holy shit, are you really in an actual relationship? My sister? Wow," he murmurs.

I cross my arms over my chest defensively. "I'm trying to be," I say. "Not that you bitches made this any easier."

He laughs. My older brother, one of the men I grew up with, someone I looked to as an example, *laughs* at my struggles.

"Becca, you are more headstrong than all of us put together. Don't pretend like you haven't always done things exactly the way you wanted to," he tells me, swirling the ice in his now-empty glass.

"That may be true, but you guys really messed me up. I feel like I have no idea what respect looks like to 'normal' people," I insist.

Chris shakes his head. "You put a lot of

stock into things you heard," he replies. "We were stupid teenagers. We would never say those kinds of things about women now. It's not exactly like you saw any of us in real relationships."

"Except you just screwed your boss and ended up back here, tail between your legs," I reply.

He looks at me levelly. "Wow, well, I think I'm going to go take a shower now. Before I yell at my little sister for making assumptions about things she knows nothing about." He rises, anger clearly written all over his face.

"I'm sorry, Chris," I say. "I'm just having a hard time. And I'm trying to understand how I got here."

He considers me for a moment before sitting back down.

"Kate and I dated off and on for the better part of a year. I asked her to be my girlfriend, to really give it a shot. I was in love with her," he explains quietly.

"Oh, Chris," I breathe.

He waves a hand. "I don't need pity," he grumbles. "It's not the first time I've been in love, and it won't be the last. But it's never easy,

Becca. It's always a risk. And Mom and Dad are proof that somehow even the most dysfunctional relationships can work, if it's with the right person. The way they are? It's weird, yeah. But it is what it is, and somehow it works for them. There is no one model for a perfect relationship. It's just loving someone enough to get up every day and decide to be with that person. Despite all the weirdness. Or maybe because of it, I don't know. That's it."

Dad chooses that moment to enter the dining room, freshly showered and holding a glass of lemonade. But I can't help noticing that his shirt buttons are done up all wrong. When Mom follows him in a moment later, her clothes are slightly disheveled and her hair is damp at the ends.

I shake my head and cover my face. Chris bursts out laughing at my reaction.

"What did we miss?" Dad asks, settling into the chair at the head of the table.

I peek through my fingers to see the most fake innocent expression ever on his face, and it sends me into gales of laughter as well. Chris and I laugh until we're crying, while our parents stare at us like we're nuts.

"Well, this is fun," Mom eventually says. "Are you staying for dinner?" Her question is directed at me, so I compose myself enough to respond.

Wiping at the tears of laughter, I nod. "Yeah, I think I'd like that, thanks, Mom."

She gives me a small smile and a quizzical look before patting my shoulder and rising.

"I'll go get started, then. If you still wanted to chat, you can come help," she offers.

"I think I'm good," I say, giving Chris a smile. "But I'll help anyway."

Dad gives me a bewildered look as I follow Mom into the kitchen, while Chris smirks. And while I end up keeping the conversation with my mother light, telling her only general things about Vincent and me, I feel like I got what I came for.

17

*A*fter the visit to my parents' house, I spend a lot of time thinking about what Chris said. About what Avery said. About what I want to do about it all.

I decide pretty quickly that Jules was right: I was afraid of becoming my mother. Well, having a relationship like my mother's and father's, because I'm so much like my mom. But what Chris said makes a lot of sense. You find something that works for you. It doesn't matter what it looks like to everyone else.

I thought I'd been in love once. It was when I was eighteen. I'd been on a few dates with a guy over the course of a few weeks. We talked a lot on the phone too, even though we only managed to meet up those few times. That should've been my first clue.

He was about ten years older than me, and I found him not only attractive but fascinating. He'd traveled to exotic places, dined at the best restaurants, moved in social circles I could only dream of. But it turned out I was one of many women, or girls, as it were, that he was seeing. And by "seeing," I mean "fucking." I wasn't a woman then, despite what I thought. But now, at twenty-six, I feel like I'm *really* in love for the first time.

And the fact that there are things about Vincent that I don't know give me pause and make me feel like I made a bad decision. Until I realized it wasn't a decision at all — I didn't decide to fall in love with him, I just did. Lord knows I'm impulsive, but I also don't get serious. And in all honesty, if I could've chosen who to get serious about — with my head — it would *not* have been Vincent DeMarco.

I knew from the start he had "bad boy" written all over him. But that's just a label. And you fall for a person, not a type.

He's surprised me on many levels. But I can't discount my concerns. And that Avery's story might not just be a story. Though that doesn't mean there isn't more to it.

While I consider all of this, I put off seeing Vincent. But by Tuesday, when he texts again asking to hang out, I've decided the time has come to just talk to him about it. Otherwise, it's going to haunt me, make me question myself, make me act in ways I don't want to. I may have dated around, but I don't play games. And I'm into this way too deep to screw around.

Thankfully, Sasha is busy with her own relationship, preparing for her last finals, and finishing her degree. Jules is once again all wrapped up in hospital business. And Harper is busy with Mason, not that we're as close anyway. So nobody pushes me about how things are going, why I'm so quiet all of a sudden and all that.

Even so, I'm a bundle of nerves on Tuesday night as I wait for Vincent to show up at my place. I'd asked him to come here rather than going out so we could talk privately. Assuming I can keep it from turning into a sex-fest, which is what I'm sure he was expecting with that sort of invitation. Normally, he'd be right.

When he knocks, I open the door, immediately proven right. He's wearing a tight black tee that hugs his muscled frame, with low-slung, fitted jeans that show off his thick thighs and, I'm sure, his gorgeous ass. Oozing sex appeal, he smolders in a way that's practically irresistible before he even says a word.

"Hey," I say, trying to sound casual but barely squeaking out the word.

A sly smirk appears on his face, like he thinks I've been struck dumb by his hotness. Again, normally he'd be right.

"Hey, yourself," he replies. "So, you gonna let me in, or what?"

I realize I've been standing fully in the doorway, blocking his entry, so I step back.

"Of course, yeah, come in," I say, feeling a blush creep up my neck. Seriously? I do not embarrass easily. This is going to be harder than I thought.

I close the door and follow him to the couch. He sinks into his usual spot in the corner, but I don't settle in his lap like I usually would. Instead, I sit down next to him, facing him with my leg tucked under me.

"I need to ask you something," I say plainly.

He sits up a little, a look of concern flitting

over his features before he quickly smooths his face back to a neutral expression.

"Sure, of course, what's up?" He's trying to sound cool, casual. But I can tell he's just as nervous as I am.

I take a deep breath. "Were you in National City last Wednesday after work?" I ask.

Whatever he was expecting, it clearly wasn't that based on the look of surprise on his face.

"Wow. Um. Yes … yes, I was," he replies slowly. "Why?"

Well, he didn't deny it. So that means at least the first part of Avery's story is true. Shit.

"I thought you had to check in with your parole officer?"

"I did. And then I went to visit a friend," he says simply, with no further explanation.

My brows pull together. "You made it sound like checking in was going to take longer. Since, you know, you said you couldn't make it to have dinner with Sasha and Cal. But you could go hang out at a friend's house for a couple of hours?"

His whole body stiffens. "How do you even know where I was, and for how long? What the hell is going on here, Becca?" His immediate defensiveness makes my stomach drop. People are only defensive when they have something to defend.

"Someone told me they saw you."

"Yeah? Who?" he asks.

"It doesn't matter. Is your 'friend' a prostitute?" I ask plainly.

He scoffs. "Is that was your source told you?" he returns in an accusatory tone. "That I was cheating on you with a prostitute?"

I consider that for a moment. "Cheating would imply we're exclusive. Which we've never actually agreed to be," I allow. "But yeah, basically, that's what they said."

"I don't know what kind of guy you think I am," he replies coldly, "but I don't cheat. Whether we've agreed to be exclusive or not, I haven't fucked anyone else. And I don't *ever* pay for sex. But what pisses me off the most is that you felt the need to even ask me that."

"I didn't ask you if you paid for or fucked a prostitute," I reply hotly. "I asked if the person you were visiting was also a prostitute. There's a difference." I don't miss that he said he hasn't *fucked* anyone else. Not that he hasn't dated anyone else.

"Please. I can read between the lines," he retorts.

"You know what I love about this conversation? That you didn't actually deny that the person you visited is a prostitute," I point out. "Or that you're not dating them or something."

He rises from the couch. "I don't need to sit here and listen to this. You either trust me, or you don't."

Sick of hearing that phrase, even though it wasn't from him before, I stand up to face him, hands on my hips. "Are you telling me if someone saw me go into some pimp's house or something, you wouldn't want to know what was going on?"

"Gigolo," he corrects. "A male prostitute is a gigolo. And no, I would trust you if you told me nothing was going on."

"Wow. *Someone* seems to know a lot about prostitutes," I snap. Even though I know I shouldn't have said it, right now I don't care. "And trusting that nothing was going on and wanting to know why I was there in the first place aren't the same thing. All I asked is where you were and who you were with."

"That. That right there is what I don't need.

Someone who wants to know where I am and who I'm with at all times. You don't trust me. Message received. I think we're done here," he says.

"Seriously? You blow me and my friends off to go hang out with someone you didn't even tell me about, and I'm not allowed to ask questions about that?" I press. "If that's over the line, then yes, I think we're done here." I cross my arms over my chest and glare up at him.

He rubs the heels of his hands into his eyes before dropping them back to his sides and looking at me imploringly.

"Okay, fine, I get why you'd have questions," he finally allows. "But do you trust that I'm not dating, fucking, or whatever with this person? That I just don't want to include you in every detail of my life all the time?" The pain on his face cuts through me like a knife.

"I do," I say. "I trust that. But that explanation doesn't make me feel any better, because now I'm worried that we're not on the same page. Because if there are parts of your life you want to keep me out of, maybe this isn't that serious to you."

"Says the woman who didn't want me to

have dinner at her parents' house on Saturday," he replies.

"I ..." Well, fuck. He's not wrong, but it's not for the reasons he thinks. "I do want you to meet my parents, there were just some things I had to take care of." He stares at me pointedly. "Yeah, okay, I get it."

"Do you?" he asks in earnest. "Because this is serious to me. I wouldn't be with you if it weren't, and I thought you knew that. But you gotta give it time. I can't give everything all at once. Believe me, I wish I could."

His explanation tugs at something inside of me. Well, several somethings. On one hand, he's absolutely right, and I knew all of that on some level. On the other hand, I can't help feeling like there's still something off about all of this. All of his deflecting and defensiveness just doesn't sit well. There's more to this story, and it feels important somehow.

But I remember what Chris said about a relationship being a choice. And my heart's made the choice for me. If I don't try to see it through, I'll always regret it.

"Okay," I say softly, my defensive stance melting.

He blanches. "Okay?"

I look up at him. "Yes. Okay. Can we stop fighting now and have makeup sex?"

He looks down at me, a muscle in his jaw ticking. His hands reach up to cup my face, and he steps toward me so our bodies are touching.

"You mean so much to me, Becca, you have no idea," he says, his forehead dipping to meet mine. His lips follow, sliding over my mouth in earnest.

I reach up, wrapping my arms around his neck as I open to him. Needing his kiss, his touch, to erase the feelings of unease that linger.

What I don't do is say the words he just said back to him. Because it's too close to "I love you." Something I want to say. But I couldn't bear not to hear it back. Not right now. Instead, I stick to what I know. I let him slowly undress me in my living room, while I slowly undress him. I let him ease me onto the couch. I let him inside me. When I come, when we come together, it feels like surrendering on every level.

18

*A*t the beginning of the day Wednesday, Vincent's words ring through my head, and something still just doesn't sit right with me. Unfortunately, the more I think about it, the more my sense of unease grows. By the end of the day, I'm a nervous wreck.

After work, I sit in my car, rocking back and forth, my mind flipping through everything we'd said to each other. When it occurs to me, I never asked if he planned to visit the friend again tonight. Yet somehow, I assumed he would. Why did I assume that?

I search my memory for any clue or reason and come up empty. Just because he checks in with the parole office every Wednesday doesn't mean he goes to that person's house every Wednesday. But I can't ignore the gut feeling that I'm right, that he's going there again today, even after our argument, and that that's why I'm so worked up. It also occurs to me that I don't need to take Avery's suggestion of following him. She gave me the address. I can simply go there. If he never shows, nothing lost. And if he does … well, I could ruin his trust forever. But I could also learn what he's hiding.

Unfortunately, I'm a risk-taker through and through. Especially if it puts me in a place of power. And knowledge is power. *That.* That is why I feel so off — I feel powerless not knowing. My impulsiveness gets the better of me, and I pull the piece of paper I'd crumpled into my pocket and rediscovered later out of my purse. The fact that I even kept it tells me I was always going to do this at some point. I know it's a stupid move. But clearly, on some level I always knew I'd use the information.

It's not a long drive, but every second, every inch, feels like eternity. When I finally spot the house, I drive by, getting a good look at the plain, one-story blue rambler with chain-link fencing. There's an old Ford Focus in the driveway and a few toys scattered in the yard. I circle the block and find a spot to park down the street that's close enough to see the house but far enough to escape notice.

After sitting in the car for ten minutes, a sharp rap on my window nearly scares me to death. I look up to find Avery, arms crossed, somehow looking both annoyed and intrigued.

I roll down the window.

"Goddamn, Avery, you nearly made me shit my pants," I chastise her.

"I see you took my advice," she says smugly. "But this is where he parks, and if he's here at the same time as last week, it'll be any minute now. Go down to the other side of the street if you don't want lover boy to see you. I'll be inside," she points at the nondescript gray house behind her, "with popcorn." Giving me another superior look, she turns and leaves without waiting for a response.

I don't hesitate, doing exactly as she suggested, even though now I feel even dirtier for this whole operation. Knowing Avery is going to witness whatever goes down is almost enough to make me abort the whole thing. Almost.

But I don't get time to second guess myself. Vincent pulls up mere moments after I've settled in my new spot. Fuck. I *knew* it.

I watch him get out of his car, look around, and walk up to the front door. It opens, but I don't get a look at the person inside before he walks in.

He's been in there a good half an hour before I start to wonder what my plan was going to be. Spoiler alert: I didn't have one.

Do I go up to the house while he's there and try to look inside? Too creepy, and someone might call the cops if I look like I'm prowling around.

Do I just go up and knock on the door? That idea has merit. If the person he's visiting answers, I might be able to learn something just by seeing them. But if he saw me ... I decide I'd rather avoid that. So my best bet, really, is to approach the house after he's gone. Maybe pretend to be selling something.

Or I could find my sanity and just go home right now. Because I'm fairly certain I've lost my damn mind.

Unfortunately, Vincent comes out a few minutes later, gets in his car, and leaves. After being there for not quite forty-five minutes. Enough time to … well, to do a lot of things. My stomach turns, and before I can find my senses, I'm out of the damn car and headed for the house. I hope Avery enjoys the show.

As I walk, I concoct a quick story in my head starring the church I'd passed on my way in. Here goes nothing.

I don't notice any signs of security as I approach. The gate is unlocked, there's no doorbell camera or anything else that I can see. That's good, at least.

I knock, and it doesn't take long for the door to open. An attractive older woman who looks to be in her forties answers the door. She's got dyed platinum blond hair and wears a fitted, leopard-print pantsuit that looks expensive on her svelte frame. If she's a hooker, she's a classy one.

"Hi," I greet her with a huge, fake smile. "I'm with St. Mary's Catholic Church, and we're looking for donations of clothing or household goods for our first rummage sale of the summer. Do you have anything you'd like to give?"

I want to smack myself. What in god's name am I doing?

The woman eyes me up and down. "I go to St. Mary's, and I don't remember them saying anything about a rummage sale," she replies suspiciously.

My heart pounds in my chest.

"Oh, it's something that the singles groups are doing," I reply, trying not to sound caught out.

"What'd you say your name was?" she asks, still clearly not buying it.

My brain scrambles for a fake name, but I'm clearly not good at this because before I can stop myself, I reply, "I'm Becca." And I hold out my damn hand. *Becca, the complete moron.*

Her eyes widen a fraction. And I know I've been caught.

"You're —"

But before she can finish her sentence, a little boy around two years old toddles up and tugs at her pants. "Come play," he insists.

Then he turns toward me. And I'd know those features anywhere: Vincent's luscious dark hair, his deep, dark eyes, his brow line, his nose ... this kid has them all, in the cutest, most angelic little package I've ever seen. And I can't help the gasp that escapes me.

I look back up at the woman in horror.

She looks down at the little boy. "Go play, sugar, I'll be right there, promise," she tells him sweetly.

I work to find my words. "I'm sorry, I didn't mean to bother you, I should —"

She reaches out and grabs my arm. "You shouldn't be here. It won't work out well for you." Her expression is inscrutable.

I want to say it already hasn't worked out well for me. Vincent has a child with this woman. Talk about huge secrets. What else don't I know? How far down does this rabbit hole go?

"I don't think you'll have to worry about that," I promise her, trying to hold back tears. Because I'm going to have to tell Vincent I was here. One way or another, this discovery is going to end our relationship.

I turn to head back down the walkway. Only to see Vincent himself, coming back up the side-walk toward the gate holding a shopping bag. He freezes in place when he sees me. I stop, and the tears come pouring out, despite myself.

"Becca, what the fuck are you doing here?" His feet restart, and he pushes through the gate, stopping right in front of me.

I've never heard him sound so angry. And even though I know he has every right to be, I'm instantly equally furious.

"I had to know. And I'm glad I came. Now I see what you've been hiding. *Who* you've been hiding. How far does this go? Are you two married? Do you live here, just a happy little family? Is that why we never go to your place? How big of a joke am I to you, Vincent?" The words tumble out without any effort, any recollection of forming them.

"We can't talk about this here, Becca. Get out of here, now," Vincent replies harshly.

"Why, so you can get me alone, whisper your sweet nothings, make me buy your story?" I say back angrily. "Not gonna happen. I'm not buying what you're selling anymore, asshole."

"Fuck," I hear loudly from behind me. The older woman has appeared back in the doorway. "Georgie's off early and on the way home, Vincent. You both need to get out of here."

Vincent suddenly looks terrified.

"Oh, so you're *not* together?" I ask. "She's

already married. I see. Yeah, wouldn't want the husband to come home and find her lover here. Figure out that their kid looks *exactly like you*."

"You saw Elijah?" he gasps, eyes wide.

I close my eyes, tears trickling over my cheeks. Such a perfect name for that adorable little saint.

"Yes. But don't worry, I'd never do something against the best interest of that little boy," I promise. "Just do me a favor and lose my phone number, would you?"

As I walk past him and out of the gate, a small coupe pulls up in front of the house. The driver steps out, and it's not a jealous husband, just a young woman with long honey-blond hair. She looks at me, confused, then her eyes land on Vincent behind me.

The pure rage in her eyes is my first clue that something is seriously wrong.

19

"What are you doing here, Vinnie, and who the fuck is this?" the girl snaps as she slings a beat-up purse over her shoulder. She looks to be in her late teens and is wearing a waitress uniform.

"I don't know, some chick," he says, sauntering up next to me and giving me a look like he's never seen me before, then turning his lazy gaze back to her. "And I think you know why I'm here, Georgette."

Georgette ... Georgie. Not the older woman's husband. Her ... daughter? I look between her and Vincent, realizing that I had it wrong. The older woman isn't Elijah's mother, this girl is.

"Becca, dear, I have those donations for you," a voice rings from behind me just as the pieces click into place in my mind. I turn to see the woman who'd answered the door walking down the path, holding a black garbage bag. She stops right in front of me and all but shoves it in my arms. "You tell Pastor Flynn I said hello, and I'll see you both at mass this Sunday." She gives me a tight smile that clearly says, *Now get the fuck out of here.*

But if she thinks it's that easy to get rid of me, she's sorely mistaken. Especially with "Vinnie" glaring daggers at me while his girlfriend isn't looking.

"Ma, what the hell?" Georgie snaps, grabbing the bags out of my arms. "You know I want to resell anything you used to donate. I need the money more than your stupid church. And what the fuck is he," she points at Vincent, "doing here? I told you he's not allowed to see Elijah."

Georgie's mom holds her hands up. "I don't know, that's between you two," she says airily, stepping back toward the porch. As she moves, her glance shoots back to me, still frozen in place on the sidewalk. "Becca, dear, you can run along now."

Georgie's head whips back to me and scans me up and down as her mother ducks back into the house. Fucking coward.

"You're wearing scrubs," she says acidly. "You're not here to see my mother. You're here with *him*, aren't you?" She gets up in my face, looking like she's about to push me.

"You need to back up off me right now," I say, hands flying to my hips.

Vincent steps between us, putting his back to me and pressing Georgie away. "Leave her alone, she's got nothing to do with this." His voice is filled with quiet menace, and a chill runs down my back.

The bitch *hisses* at him like a fucking cat. I freeze in place, the anger at her challenge totally replaced by fear of getting in the middle of this argument. I don't even try to sneak away, for fear of making it worse. Because clearly this bitch is cray-cray.

"This is the trash you're with now?" she screeches. I bristle at this bitch calling *me* trash but manage to keep my mouth shut. "And you think you can just bring her here *and* see Elijah behind my back? I warned you, Vinnie —"

"I didn't bring her here," he interrupts her angrily. "And he's my fucking kid too, Georgie. You can't make me stay away from him just because I don't want to be with you."

More pieces drop into place at his words. The reason for his sneaking around. For keeping secrets. He's not just a dad; he's a dad to a kid with a psycho bitch for a mom. A psycho bitch who clearly isn't about to let him go without a fight.

"Like hell I can't," she screams. "He's *mine*. I can do whatever I want. I told you, you leave, don't come back. We're a package deal. It's both of us, or neither. You know the deal."

"You can't *do* that, Georgie," he grinds out angrily.

I peek around Vincent's broad back and watch her step up to him, glowering.

"Watch me," she says. Then she turns and runs into the house.

Vincent whirls on me, looking more tortured than I've ever seen him.

"You couldn't just fucking trust me?" he barks at me. "You had to follow me here?"

"Apparently, I was one hundred percent right

not to trust you," I point out. "Considering this massive part of your life you've been keeping from me." Deep down, I don't want to fight about this with him. I just want to run.

He crosses his arms over his broad chest. "You have no idea what you've started," he mutters, shaking his head. "You should get out of here while you can."

"*I've* started? She would've found you here whether I showed up or not," I scoff. "How the fuck is any of this my fault?" Like hell I'm going to take the blame for this. For *his* secrets. Even though, on some level, I get why he didn't tell me. But I don't want to think about that right now. All I know is the hurt I'm feeling.

He runs a hand through his hair, agitated, and opens his mouth to reply, but is cut off by the front door of the house bursting open. Georgie comes out, dragging a crying Elijah by one hand, a duffel bag in the other.

"Mommy, noooo," Elijah screams. His little wail breaks my heart in half. Something about the kid just gets me right in the chest.

"Shut up," she snaps at him, glaring daggers at Vincent and I as she storms past us. She throws the bag in the trunk, then puts Elijah in the car seat in the back while Vincent stares with wide eyes. My chest feels tight, and I fight the urge to stop her. As if sensing my tension, Vincent puts an arm up to hold me back.

"Where the fuck are you going?" he demands, finally finding his voice.

The petite blonde slams the door shut and saunters up to him.

"I'm leaving. With Elijah. Same deal, Vinnie," she says in a deceptively soft voice. "You can have it all," she bats her eyelashes up at him, "or nothing." She takes a step back and turns to open the driver's side door. "Last chance."

Georgie's mother appears next to me. "Don't do this," she pleads with her daughter.

Vincent takes a step toward the car so he stands between me and his ex, then looks back at me with regret in his eyes. Georgie stares at him expectantly.

It's the moment of truth. Will he go with her? This woman who clearly holds the key to a past I knew nothing about until today? A past I've been trying to pry out of him for as long as I've known him? Or will he choose to stay here, with me? A woman he's known a fraction of his child's life. A woman whose trust he's broken? I'm no genius, but I know what I'd do.

Vincent turns back to her, closing the distance between them. His hand slips under her chin, tipping her face up to look into his and, despite my anger, my hurt, and the betrayal I feel, my heart breaks seeing him touch her like that.

"I swore I'd always be there for our son," he says. It's quiet, but I can still hear every word. Hell, you could hear a fucking pin drop. It's like the world has held its breath in this moment. "But nothing's changed between us, Georgie, and you can't make me be with you so I can see my kid. And I'm not going to let you take him."

Just as the knot in my chest unravels the tiniest bit, the soft expression on her face melts into tight rage. With a sudden, swift movement, she knees him in the balls.

He doubles over, crying out in pain, and she takes the chance to get in the car, snapping the locks shut behind her. I roll my eyes. I could've told him she'd do that.

Georgie's mother unfreezes beside me, striding quickly down the walk to the car window, around a still-bent-over Vincent. She bangs a hand on Georgie's window.

"Stop this right now, young lady," she calls sternly.

Georgie flips her off and starts the car, just as Vincent manages to pull himself back up. Quickly, he skirts to the front of the car, putting his hands on the hood.

I watch in horror as they have a staring match standoff. The man I love, despite everything, and a crazy bitch behind the wheel of a two-ton-plus vehicle. With their child in the backseat. What insane, fucked-up parallel universe have I landed in?

In a move nobody expected, Georgie *backs out* of the spot down the street, and Vincent almost falls flat on his face. Georgie's mother and I gasp simultaneously. Georgie guns the engine, but Vincent barely has time to right himself, much less move, when the car shoots forward, gaining speed fast. He's not standing far from the curb, but the car swerves just enough to hit him as it goes past.

My heart stops as I watch his body fly over the hood of the car on the driver's side as she continues to accelerate forward, rolls off to the side, and lands in a heap on the street as she drives off.

Without a thought, I hurtle forward to him. I streak past Georgie's mom, who stands, stunned on the sidewalk.

"Call 911," I command as I make it to Vincent's prone form.

He lays on his back, unconscious. His jeans are torn, his legs obviously badly damaged as the left one is sitting at an odd angle, though I can't see anything more than a scrape. I scramble up to his head, moving to examine the back side, which is in contact with the pavement. I see a small pool of blood steadily growing larger.

A low moan from the sidewalk catches my attention. I look up at the panicking woman, who fumbles with her phone.

"Oh my god," another voice cries. Avery runs up from my other side, settling down next to me. "I saw everything. What can I do?"

I look at Georgie's' mom, who still hasn't managed to place the call.

"Call 911," I tell her. "I've got him."

Avery nods and quickly pulls out her phone and dials.

I sit down on the pavement behind Vincent's head and remove my scrubs top. Thankfully, I have a tank top on underneath. I carefully brace his head and neck and lift so I can scoot my knees under him. With his shoulders resting on my knees, I roll my shirt and hold it gently on the back of his head wound while I hold the weight of his head with my other hand to keep his head and neck straight and supported.

My eyes flick back up at Avery's voice, now clearly talking to a dispatcher.

"They want to know if he's breathing," she tells me.

I nod. "He's breathing but unconscious. Head trauma with bleeding, likely skull fracture, and possible spinal damage, as well as contusions and possible fractures to the lower extremities. I have his head and neck in a stable position, but we need an ambulance *now*."

I focus on my emergency training, breathing steadily as I maintain gentle pressure to contain the bleeding. If I press too hard, any fractured pieces of skull could penetrate, causing even more damage.

Don't think about that, Becca, I tell myself. *Breathe. Focus. Stay steady.*

Avery puts a hand on my shoulder, and it's strangely reassuring. I hear her relaying the information, continuing to talk to the person on the phone as we wait. I vaguely recall that Paradise Valley Hospital is probably three minutes away by ambulance. I'm trying to focus on that fact when Vincent's eyes flutter and open, and my heart skips.

"Hey," I say soothingly, relief flooding through me. If he's already conscious, there's hope that the head trauma isn't as bad as it could be. "I need you to stay perfectly still, okay? You were just hit, and an ambulance is on the way."

He blinks hard but doesn't respond.

"Blink again if you heard me, okay?" I ask.

He blinks.

"Tell her he's conscious and responsive," I call to Avery. I hear her relay the information and take a subtle breath before addressing Vincent again. "You're going to be okay, do you hear me?"

He blinks. I feel tears prick the backs of my eyes. I hear sirens in the distance. *Thank god.*

I can't help glancing up to look for the ambulance, and my eyes fall on Georgie's mother. Her hand is still clenched around her phone as she stares helplessly at the three of us. I try not to let anger take over. I still need to focus on keeping Vincent still. But damn, bitch couldn't — or wouldn't — even call for help. Who are these people and how did Vincent ever get involved with them?

Moments later, a police car appears down the road, followed by an ambulance.

"Avery," I say softly, my eyes flicking to hers.

She nods. "I'm here. What do you need?"

I glance over at Georgie's mom, who looks like she wants to run. "Make sure the cops know what happened, that they talk to her," I gesture with my head toward the shocked older woman, "and that her daughter has potentially illegally abducted the son she has with Vincent."

Avery's eyes go wide, and I suddenly hate that I have to trust her right now. But there's nothing more important than making sure Vincent and his son are both okay. There's a sentence I never thought I'd say.

I'm distracted from my concerns as the medics arrive, and I work with them to get Vincent into a neck brace, onto a stretcher, and hooked up to oxygen to minimize chances of further damage. Once they're loading him into the ambulance, I turn back to Avery, who is talking with one of the police officers.

I join them at the squad car and see Georgie's mom sitting there, though she's uncuffed.

"They're taking her in to give a statement," Avery explains quietly as the officer turns to talk to his partner.

"And you?" I ask.

"I'll give one too, but I can join you at the hospital first if you need someone there with you," she offers.

"Wow. Um. Thank you. That's … surprisingly nice of you," I admit. "But I'll be okay. Is there any way you can go with them and bring her to me when you're done? I'd like to have a little chat with her."

"I'll try. They're going to want a statement from you too."

I nod. "I know." One of the medics calls that they're ready to go. "I'll be at Paradise Valley. I can do it from there."

Avery reaches out and gives my hand a squeeze. "I'm so sorry about this, Becca. About everything, really. I didn't think anything like this would happen, I swear."

I give her a vague, tired smile. "Thanks, but it's not your fault." The medic calls out again. "Gotta go."

Without waiting for a response, I turn and bound toward the ambulance, hopping into the front seat while the other medic pulls the back door closed behind him. The driver gives me a sympathetic smile before flicking on the lights and sirens.

I lean back into the seat for the short ride, trying to breathe through the distress of the last minutes.

"You a nurse?" the driver asks, eyeing my scrubs.

"Medical assistant," I correct. "At Rutherford."

He nods. "Then you know your friend is going to be fine. Vitals looked good."

"How were his legs?" I ask. It's the one thing I didn't have time to check, what with making sure he didn't bleed out on the pavement.

"Left femur is definitely fractured. Contusions on both legs. Pelvis seemed stable, though," he replies succinctly.

I nod. "Good." All easily treated and healed. As long as the skull fracture isn't too bad, all things considered, it could have been much worse.

But for once, I don't say any of the million things that are on my mind. Because when I do, I'll have to think about the big, brown eyes of that little boy as his mother threw him into the back of that car. As much as I care about Vincent, the idea of something happening to his son because of all this ... I shake myself, unwilling to *what if* myself into a panic attack. One thing at a time.

Thankfully, we arrive at the emergency room before I can think too hard, and I accompany them as they wheel Vincent in through the emergency doors. Once he's handed off to the ER team, though, I have no choice but to stay the reception area. I'm not family, and even if I were, right now the hospital staff need to do their jobs. I know that better than anyone.

Unfortunately, I don't even have enough information about him to fill out the forms. It's a huge slap-in-the-face realization how little I really know Vincent DeMarco.

Thirty agonizing minutes later, Avery arrives with a police officer … and Georgie's mother, who at least looks chagrined at this point.

I give my statement to the officer while Avery hangs on every word. I don't try to stop her. At this point she's at least earned the right to hear what I know. She did help at a critical moment, after all.

I thank her for helping, and she leaves with such little fanfare that I'm starting to think maybe she's not all bad. Not that I plan to be friends with her after all the shit she pulled. But it's enough to ratchet down the animosity that had been raging between us. So that's something.

I'm left in the waiting room, just me and Georgie's mother. I slink into a seat next to her.

"I hate to have to ask you this, but is there anyone else we should call? Vincent's dad? Does he have any other family here?" I ask.

She shakes her head. "He's got no one here besides me," she replies. "I don't know about his dad."

I sigh. The little I know tells me even if his

dad cared, he's still in Queens, so there's not much he could do. And he and Vincent aren't exactly close, anyway. I decide against calling Mason for now, unsure of how much he knows about this situation. I don't want to do anything to make it even worse.

"So, what's your name?" I ask. She looks up at me with tired eyes. "Because I keep calling you 'Georgie's mom' in my head. Might be easier if I actually knew what to call you."

"Crystal," she offers quietly.

"Crystal," I repeat back. Seems more like a stripper name than a hooker name, but what do I know? "So the officer told me they haven't found Georgie and Elijah yet."

She presses her lips together and sighs. "I don't know where she is," she says defensively.

I give her a hard stare. The woman did allow Vincent to see his son against her daughter's wishes. But Georgie is still her daughter.

"Would you tell me if you did?" I ask.

The indignation in her eyes is real. "Absolutely," she insists. "Georgie can't take care of that little boy on her own. And no matter what you think of me, I love my grandson."

I gathered as much, since she was clearly

trying to get rid of me before her daughter realized who I was. Or, who I was to Vincent, as it were.

"Wait, what do you mean, *can't*?" I ask.

Crystal gives me a reluctant glance. "Georgie has some mental health issues," she admits. "It's not her fault."

Well, that's one way to shut down questions, even though now I have a million more. I consider that for a minute before asking my next question.

"Why didn't you call 911 when I asked you to?" I ask, purposely switching the topic.

And also because, while I was waiting, I realized it might be because she's trying to protect her daughter, which clearly she is. Or it could also be because she's had enough run-ins with the law not to want to involve them. Either way, I'm curious.

"I wanted to," she says slowly. "I just … froze. The situation with Vincent … it's complicated."

I look at her in disgust. "So complicated that you wanted him to bleed out on the damn street?"

"No," she says forcefully. "I knew the police

would come too. And that Georgie would try to use this against him again. I didn't want that for him. But I would've called if your friend hadn't."

"In the future, you should know that minutes count," I snap. "He could've died by the time you figured out your shit. Thank god Avery was there." Through my anger, her words sink in. "Wait, *again?*"

"The history between my daughter and your boyfriend is very long, and very complicated," she replies.

"Well, try to use short, simple sentences, and I might be able to keep up," I reply sarcastically.

She huffs a dry laugh. "You should really ask Vincent. It's his story to tell. But for my part, obviously, I thought he had a right to see his son. Georgie didn't agree, and it's caused … friction. Between her and I. Between her and Vincent. On top of everything else, my daughter is extremely stubborn. It's her best and worst quality."

A woman in scrubs appears through the double doors and approaches.

"You're here for Vincent DeMarco?" she asks.

We both rise and nod. "He's stable now," she tells us. "He has a broken leg, two broken ribs, and a minor skull fracture with no brain damage. He's going to be just fine. You can see him now if you'd like."

Crystal looks at me nervously. "I really shouldn't, I don't want to upset him," she hedges.

I glare at her. "He's going to have questions I may not be able to answer. You're coming with me," I insist.

She shrugs in acceptance, and we follow the nurse to a semiprivate room with an empty second bed. Vincent sits propped up in the other, his head and chest wrapped tightly in bandages, his left leg propped up in a fresh cast from hip to ankle.

I tap his IV bag with a small smile.

"Hope they're giving you some good drugs," I say by way of greeting.

He reaches out to squeeze my hand.

"You're pretty," he says.

I can't help laughing. "That's a big yes," I tease.

He smiles, but it doesn't reach his eyes. "I was kidding," he explains. "But yeah, I'm good." His eyes move to Crystal. "Where is she? Where's Elijah?"

Crystal shakes her head helplessly and doesn't respond.

"The police are looking for them," I supply. "Don't worry, Vincent, they'll find them. They're going to come talk to you soon."

He snorts. "The cops? Great, that's the last thing I need right now."

I furrow my brow before remembering he's on parole.

"You can't possibly be in any trouble because of this," I say.

He looks up at me, then looks at Crystal. "You want to tell her about the last time I got in trouble with the police?"

Crystal flushes beet red.

I look between them, confused.

"I'll tell them," she finally says. "I've let her get away with too much. I'm sorry, Vincent. I should've told them sooner."

"Told who what?" I ask, still puzzled.

Vincent snorts. "I wasn't even sure you really knew until just now," he admits, bitterness filling his words. "But I guess that answers that question."

Crystal settles on the bed next to him, squeezing his hand so hard her knuckles turn white. "There's more at stake for me than you know, but Elijah is more important."

"Someone want to fill me in here, or should I leave you two to have a moment?" I ask crossly. Even though I have no right to be the upset party right now.

Crystal rises from the bed and faces me. "I think Vincent can fill you in from here. I need to go amend my statement to the police," she replies. "Anything I can do to make what comes next … well, not as much of a shitshow. For Elijah."

"For Elijah," Vincent says pointedly.

She swallows hard and nods resolutely before leaving the room.

Vincent and I stare at each other silently.

"I'm sure you're tired," I finally say. "I can go. You don't owe me an explanation."

"I kind of do," he replies. "Sit." He pats the bed next to him. I stand there, battling between deathly curious and exhausted from the drama. "Please?"

I take a seat, careful not to hurt him.

"So. You're a dad. And your ex is —"

"Trying to kill me?" he supplies.

"This isn't the first time?" I ask, surprised.

"No, it is," he assures me. "I hear it's thanks to you that she didn't succeed."

I can't help rolling my eyes. "You weren't hurt *that* bad," I reply.

"Still. Thank you."

My cheeks warm. "You're welcome. So you gonna tell me about the last time you got in trouble with the cops? The full story this time."

"The full story," he promises.

"If you feel up to it," I hedge.

His dark eyes sweep over my face for a minute before he responds. "After what just happened, I think you deserve to know." He takes a slow, deep breath. "Crystal is an escort. Not a prostitute."

My eyebrows shoot up. "There's a difference?" I ask.

"Eh," he replies, and we both laugh. "Anyway, the guy who ran her agency also ran a construction business by day. He was the boss who called the cops on me. After I broke things off with Georgie the last time."

"The last time?"

"Yeah. The last time. Lord. Guess I need to

go back further, huh?" I give him an encouraging look, and he squirms. "I met Georgie at a party in Queens. She was visiting her cousin. We hooked up and I found out once she'd gone home, she was pregnant. And she'd lied about her age. Told me she was eighteen, but she was barely seventeen. Said if I didn't move out here to take care of her and the baby, her mom was going to have me arrested."

I scoff in disbelief. "Crystal? She's terrified of involving the cops. I can't see that happening."

"Yeah, that was a lie too. Georgie just wanted to get me out here. And once I was out here, she got me a job with her 'Uncle' Nate. The first time I broke up with her, he threatened to fire me if I didn't give it another shot with her. Between that and Elijah … well, I figured it couldn't hurt to give it another go."

"Let me guess," I interject. "That didn't work out because she's … how do I say this politely? Sanity-challenged?" He smirks at me … and more pieces click together. "So he set you up and had you arrested when you wouldn't stay with her."

"Bingo," he replies. "She still let me see

Elijah for a while, and I always suspected Crystal knew about Nate setting me up, but I didn't ask. Didn't want to rock the boat."

"So what changed that?" I ask. "Georgie letting you see Elijah, I mean."

Vincent's expression darkens.

"After a while, I started seeing someone. When it got serious, I wanted to introduce her to Elijah. Georgie flipped out. I think she thought on some level that I'd come back to her. So it just totally set her off," he explains.

"Ah. So new girlfriend, no more Elijah. So you stopped having new girlfriends," I realize.

He shakes his head sadly. "I wish it were that easy. Georgie attacked Rachel. Then slit her tires for good measure. *Then* she cut me off from Elijah, telling me I'd only get to see him when I realized we were meant for each other."

The sorrow on his face rips through me. And I feel like a first-class ass for poking around for answers all this time. I can see how hard this whole situation has been on him and why I'd be the last person he'd want to tell.

"So … you didn't see things getting serious with me and thought it'd be safe, then?" I hazard. Even though that explanation makes me feel things I don't want to admit.

"God, no," he replies vehemently. "I tried, Becca. I tried not to fall for you. So fucking hard. But it was useless."

I look up into his eyes, shocked. Because it's like he's describing exactly how I felt. And now I know it wasn't just me. It reminds me how much I've come to care for him in the last month. And the last thing I want to do, even though I'm still pissed that he didn't tell me all of this sooner, is to make this harder for him.

"Me too," I admit. "But for that exact reason, I'm not going to make this more difficult for you. When they find her, I don't want to be the reason you can't see your son anymore. I'll stay away, Vincent, I promise."

"What if I don't want you to?" he asks huskily.

I close my eyes against the swell of emotion that rises in me at his words. I don't want to either. But this isn't about what I want. Hell, it's not even about what he wants.

"This isn't about that. It's about what's best for your son," I whisper. I open my eyes.

"You're right," he agrees. "But that doesn't

mean …” He trails off with a frustrated sigh. “I guess we’ll just have to see how it all plays out.”

“Guess so. Because the most important thing right now is to find them, and —” I freeze midsentence as it hits me. “I think I know where they might be.”

20

It's nearly midnight when my phone rings.

"Did they find them?"

"Hello to you too." Vincent's deep voice has a hint of laughter, and I can't help hoping that's a good thing.

"I'm on the edge of my damn seat here, and visiting hours are over so I can't come strangle you for taunting me. Spit it out already."

"Yes. They found them. Georgie is in custody for attempted manslaughter, and Elijah is with Crystal," he replies. "I don't know why I didn't think to have them check Nate's place. You're a genius, Becca, and I owe you big time."

My whole body deflates with the relief of knowing Elijah is safe.

"You don't owe me anything. I'm just glad I was able to help."

"You did more than that. Crystal told the cops she knew Nate set me up for the theft charges, and apparently Georgie has already admitted it."

"She did what, now?" I ask incredulously. "Are you serious? Why would she do that?"

"She's not in her right mind," he replies. "They're going to have her evaluated. I think they think she's on drugs, but Georgie's just messed up, Becca. I've known that for a while now."

"Damn," I say. "Well, maybe she can get the help she needs then."

"I hope so," he murmurs. "But I should let you go. You have to work tomorrow, and you've already dealt with enough drama for one day."

"Oh, I'm not going in tomorrow," I respond smugly. "I'm going to be right by your side first thing. I had another idea."

"I'd try to pry it out of you, but it sounds like you plan on holding it over my head," he teases.

"Smart *and* sounding much better already," I

reply. "I'll see you in the morning, Vincent."

***

WHEN I WALK INTO VINCENT'S HOSPITAL ROOM, the happy look he gives me quickly melts into confusion when he sees my companion.

"Hey," he greets me warily.

"Hi," I reply brightly. "Vincent, this is Ms. Suarez. She's from Child Protective Services and will be working with the DA's office on Elijah's case."

Ms. Suarez steps forward and extends a hand to Vincent, who takes it with a bewildered look.

"I'm so sorry to hear about what happened, but it sounds like your prognosis is good," she offers.

"Yeah, thanks. I'll be released in a day or two, then out of the cast six to eight weeks after that," he agrees, still looking totally unnerved. He looks at me. "I'm sorry, why is she here?"

I chuckle.

"When I gave my statement last night, I asked what would happen to Elijah. They gave me a number to call to talk to the case worker assigned. Instead, I showed up at their offices this morning and had a little chat with Ms. Suarez," I reply.

"And I wanted to speak with you directly," she offers to Vincent. "After a quick review of the case, even without the confession of attempted manslaughter, your ex-wife's —"

"We were never married," Vincent interjects sharply.

Ms. Suarez blushes. "My apologies. *Ms. Johnson's* mental health evaluation will weigh heavily in the custody matters. Her mother's statement seems to imply she won't be found mentally sound to have sole custody of Elijah," she responds.

"So, what, Crystal will?" Vincent asks.

"Is that what you want?" she asks.

"Better her than Georgie," Vincent responds with a one-shouldered shrug.

Ms. Suarez glances at me, then looks back at Vincent.

"Are you saying you don't want custody of your son, Mr. DeMarco?" she asks pointedly.

Vincent's jaw drops. "No, I ... I honestly never even thought it was an option," he admits.

"And why not?" Ms. Suarez asks.

"I have a criminal record," he replies,

looking down into his hands.

"Except that the charges against Ms. Johnson will include conspiracy to frame-up," she responds. "And since she's already confessed to it, it's just a matter of process and time until that conviction is removed from your record. And I should point out that Mrs. Johnson, her mother, also has a criminal record for solicitation, albeit in the distant past."

I smother a smile. Escort, my ass.

"What are you saying?" Vincent asks, wide-eyed.

"I'm saying that, if things go the way it appears that they will, if you wanted it, you could have sole custody of your son. Or shared with Mrs. Johnson, if that was your wish," she says plainly.

"Are you serious?" he gasps.

Ms. Suarez and I both laugh.

"Quite," she assures him.

"I … I'm just …" he stutters. "Thank you. Yes, that's what I want. Please. Oh my god." He scrubs his hands over his face, clearly in disbelief.

Ms. Suarez rises and offers a business card, which he accepts. "Then I trust we'll be speaking again soon. I wish you a speedy recovery, Mr. DeMarco," she says with a smile.

"Thank you," he says again.

Ms. Suarez gives me a nod, and I wink back. With a chuckle, she slips out the door, leaving us alone. I look back at Vincent, who is staring down at the business card in his hands.

"You okay?" I ask softly.

He looks up, his eyes swimming with tears. "So beyond fucking okay," he admits before they spill over onto his cheeks.

It makes me tear up too, and I rush to wrap my arms gently around him. "I'm sorry you had to go through all this, but I'm so happy that you'll get the chance to really be Elijah's daddy."

He pulls back, palming my face in his hand. "Thanks to you."

I shake my head. "You would've gotten here eventually. Maybe even without this," I gently touch the bandage on his head, "if I weren't around."

He wraps his hand around my fingers, drawing them to his mouth. "I don't remember you running me over with a car," he murmurs. "In fact, I'm pretty sure you're the one that held me together afterward. You're still holding me together."

I grin. "So I guess this means I don't have to stay away after all?"

"You'd better not," he replies, with a mock menacing glare.

"Yeah? Think you can put up with me for a while longer?" I tease.

His eyes turn serious. "I think the question is, do you know what you're getting into? My life's about to change, Becca. I'm going to be responsible for another human being."

I nod. "I know. You're going to be great. And I'll be right there with you."

"Seriously?"

"Seriously."

"Why?"

I take a deep breath and put my hands on either side of his face. "Because I love you, dumbass."

Vincent laughs so hard he shakes, until he grabs his side. "Ow," he exclaims.

"Sorry," I reply with a guilty look, dropping my hands.

"I love you too, you know," he says so easily that I'm shocked into silence. He stares at me expectantly. "Did I just render Becca Dillon speechless?" He starts to laugh again, then thinks better of it as he holds a hand to his side, simmering down into a low chuckle.

"I'm … yeah, I didn't expect that," I admit.

"I didn't expect *you*," he says huskily, his eyes dark and intense. "I was trying to focus on my job. My kid. Staying off Georgie's radar. Then you blew apart my life." His gaze is so tender it tears through all my usual bullshit.

A blush heats my cheeks, and I can't find words. Embarrassed and speechless. This might be a first.

"I don't know what to say to that," I admit quietly, fidgeting with the hospital blanket covering his uninjured leg. "Except … maybe, I'm sorry."

His brows pull together. "For what?"

I look up at the ceiling and work my lips between my teeth for a moment, trying to put my thoughts together. When I look back down at him, the patience and love in his eyes hits me right in the gut.

"For not trusting you. I guess I just had this … this idea in the back of my head that you were a certain type of guy," I admit.

"Yeah, I get that a lot," he replies with a grim expression.

"You don't deserve it," I respond heatedly. "And I'm such a fucking hypocrite. At the same time I assumed you'd be an awful boyfriend, I still wanted you. I couldn't see past my own bullshit assumptions. And turns out, I've got a lot of them. Hot guys are all talk. Bad boys don't make good boyfriends." I pause, nerves welling in me. "Some girls you don't take home to mom."

Vincent's eyes cloud over. "That's what you think? You're not the kind of girl a guy would want to take home?" he asks, his voice thick with emotion.

I blink back tears. "On some level, yeah," I admit. "But I didn't even realize I thought that until I figured out that I'd put a label on you that I kept trying to make you live up to. Because that's exactly what I've been doing to myself. Trying to live up to my own reputation."

"I get it," he says, taking my hands in his. "Especially at Rutherford. Man, I've never heard people talk so much shit in my life. They sure had a lot to say about you. Even before we were going out."

"Oh, lordy," I groan. "I can only imagine. Is that why you were so standoffish with me at first?"

He considers that for a moment. "Yeah, probably," he admits. "So I guess we're both guilty of believing the hype." He brings one of my hands to his mouth and places a gentle kiss on my palm. "But that was before I knew you. You're nothing like all the shit they say, Becca. You're loyal, and fierce, and a fucking goddess. My fucking goddess. If my mom was still around, I know she'd love you. Because I do."

I close my eyes, but a tear slips out anyway. I wipe it away hastily, but he grabs my hand to stop me.

"Hey," he says softly. I open my eyes to look into his. "I see you. All of you. It's what made me fall for you. Don't ever forget that."

I lean in, unable to stop myself, capturing his lips. Just to feel his mouth against mine. The warmth and connection I have with him in this moment is indescribable.

"Thank you," I whisper after breaking the kiss.

"Anytime, beautiful," he whispers back, then pulls his head farther away. He gives me a funny look. "This might be a weird time to ask … but was I hallucinating, or was Avery there last night?"

I chuckle. "Oh, you weren't hallucinating. She's the one who saw you at Crystal's last week. She's staying at her aunt's place down the block."

He groans and leans back into the stack of pillows behind him. "So I guess everyone at work already knows everything?"

I tilt my head. "I'm not so sure about that. I kind of think she'll keep her mouth shut."

"That'd be a first," he scoffs.

I snort. "True story," I agree. "Does it really matter, though? We've got each other now, bae. Doesn't matter what they say anyway."

He swipes his thumb over my cheek. "You're right. Nothing else matters."

I hear a soft knock on the door, and I pull back with a smile.

"Well, there is *one* other thing that matters," I say slyly.

Vincent raises an eyebrow.

"Come in," I call.

The door opens and Crystal peeks around it. I look down and see Elijah peering around her legs. His eyes go wide when they land on Vincent. I hear Vincent's breath catch behind me when he spots his son.

"Daddy's broken," Elijah gasps.

Crystal and I chuckle.

"I'm gonna be just fine, buddy," Vincent calls. "Come here."

Elijah looks up at Crystal, who nods in encouragement. I take a step back to give them room as Crystal follows him to the bed, helping him climb up next to Vincent. Elijah settles into the crook of his dad's arm on the uninjured side, resting his tiny hand on Vincent's broad chest.

My breath catches in my throat as Vincent plants a kiss on the little boy's head, squeezing him tightly into his body.

"I missed you, bud," he murmurs into Elijah's hair.

Elijah rolls his eyes and looks up at Vincent. "Daddy, I saw you yesterday," he huffs. "But Daddy ... Mommy was naughty." He says the last bit in a fearful whisper.

"I know," Vincent assures him. "But it's going to be okay. It's all going to be okay from now on. I promise."

My heart breaks thinking of all the drama this poor kid has been through.

"I'm going to go and let you guys have some time together," I say softly.

Vincent looks up at me.

"Stay," he says quietly. "Please."

Crystal gives me a look. "If you plan on sticking around, you should go introduce yourself," she suggests.

"Really?" I ask quietly. "You don't think it's too much right now? I don't know anything about kids. I don't want to scare him."

"Kids are resilient. Trust me," she assures me. "I'll be in the waiting room if you need me." Before I can protest, she slips out.

I approach the bed warily.

"Bud, this is my friend Becca," Vincent says to him.

I stick my hand up for a high five, which Elijah promptly smacks with his own sticky little hand.

"'Sup, dude," I greet him.

"Hello," Elijah says. "Do you like *The Octonauts*?"

I shoot Vincent an amused glance. "TV show," he mouths.

"Well, I've never seen the show, so I don't know," I tell the bright-eyed little boy looking up at me curiously. I sit down next to him. "Why don't you tell me about them?"

It was clearly the right thing to say, as Elijah launches into a stream-of-consciousness info session on what is obviously his favorite show. When he requires me to parrot something back, I happily do so, just to hear his excited little voice. And to see the glint in Vincent's eyes watching us interact.

As scared as I was of this part, it's a lot easier than I thought it would be.

We don't visit for long when Crystal comes to collect Elijah to get home for an early lunch. Once they've gone, one look at Vincent tells me he could use some rest.

"I should go too," I tell him.

"Stay just a little longer," he pleads. Then he stares at me for a moment. "I can't lie. Seeing you two together ... damn, Becca." He puts a hand to his heart, and he doesn't have to say anything else. I felt it too.

"He's a great kid, Vincent."

"Yeah, he is. But ... it's a lot. I get that. I

hope you can give it a chance, though," he says, vulnerability seeping out of him.

I sigh heavily. "Are you serious right now? He's like a little version of you. I couldn't look at that kid and not love him," I assure him. "The moment I saw him yesterday … god, I can't even with this." I wipe away tears. "Trust me, I'm not going anywhere."

"You have no fucking idea how happy I am to hear you say that," he admits. He gestures with both hands for me to come closer. I slide down next to him, folding into his uninjured side.

I look up into his eyes, more sure than ever. This is where I'm meant to be. As nuts as it seems that a little more than a month ago he was just a guy I was screwing around with. And now I can't imagine life without him.

As he looks down into my eyes, I can tell he feels the same way.

"Are we crazy?" I ask him.

"I'm crazy about you," he replies with a smirk. "And I'm so glad you know everything now. I wanted to tell you, I swear. I just didn't know how. I didn't want anything bad to happen."

I nod. "I get it. I think we're both in new territory here. But there's nobody else I'd be here with."

His dark eyes burn into mine, his mouth reaching down. I meet him with my lips, stroking mine gently against his. Keeping it light, even though it's a struggle.

He finally pulls back. "Me neither," he agrees. His eyes start to drift closed. "Becca?"

I look up again to see his head tilted toward me, his eyes closed.

"Hmmm?" I ask softly, knowing he's probably already half asleep.

"Stay," he says on a soft breath that turns into a snore.

I contain a laugh, pulling the blanket around us. I look up into his gorgeous face, an unmistakable ache in my chest.

I lean up and place a soft kiss on his cheek.

"Always," I whisper. And it feels true. Because I've never cared about anyone the way I care about him. Never loved like this. Never felt like such a fucking sap. Sasha is going to make so much fun of me. And she's going to be so damn happy.

I'm so damn happy. Because I'm pretty sure

I've found the love of my life. And like hell I'm going anywhere.

Thank you so much for reading! Please take a minute to leave a review on any retailer, goodreads, and/or BookBub. Even if it's just a couple of sentences, your opinion is important to potential readers and to me. Thank you!

Want to see more of Becca and Vincent and find out what happens between Julianna and a sexy stranger she meets at the hospital's annual gala? Get *You Can't Buy Love* (Book 3) now at https://melanieasmithauthor.com/books-you-cant-buy-love.html

Sign up for Melanie A. Smith's newsletter to get a FREE book plus all the latest news and more https://melanieasmithauthor.com/newsletter.html

ACKNOWLEDGMENTS

Thank you to the bad boys I dated long, long ago. Would that life imitated fiction, but at least they helped me realize I needed to marry the nicest guy possible. And thankfully, I did.

Which brings me to a huge thank you, as always, to my husband, for being my biggest cheerleader, sounding board, and mini-me distractor. Go team Smith!

Thank you, Lindsey Powell, my alpha reader and sister-from-another-(British)-mister. We may be separated by many miles, but you're always there to read my words, share knowledge, and talk about anything and everything.

Thank you, Erin Knuth and Jacqueline Simon Gunn, for being my beta readers. Your insight helped polish Becca and Vincent's story, and your amazing positivity and support helped me polish my confidence.

Thank you, Jenny Gardner, my badass editor

and friend of more than half my life. You freaking rock, and I'm so lucky to know you.

And, of course, a huge thank you to everyone who takes the time to read my words. It's amazing to have an outlet for the stories in my head, and even more amazing that people enjoy them.

ABOUT THE AUTHOR

Melanie A. Smith is a former engineer turned stay-at-home mom and award-winning, international best-selling author of steamy contemporary romance. She crafts strong book boyfriends with hearts of gold and smart, self-sufficient heroines. When she's not lost in the world of books, you'll find her spending time with family, cooking, and driving with the windows down and the stereo cranked up loud.

facebook.com/MelanieASmithAuthor

twitter.com/MelASmithAuthor

instagram.com/melanieasmithauthor

Tough Love

Finding His Redemption

Vegas Baby (Hot Vegas Nights)

Pompous Paramedic (A Hero Club Novel)

Short Stories

Cruising for Love

Hot for Santa

www.ingramcontent.com/pod-product-compliance
Lightning Source LLC
Chambersburg PA
CBHW021132110726
47900CB00002B/317